Redemption

'Moving on from the house that sat down'

with love
Alice May

Copyright

First Edition October 2018

ISBN: 9781 723898273
Imprint: Independently published

Copyright © October 2018 Genevieve Alice May Tomkins

All rights reserved in media

No part of this book may be used or reproduced without written permission, except in the case of brief quotations embodied in critical articles and review.

The moral right of Genevieve Alice May Tomkins to be identified as the author of this Work has been asserted by her in accordance with the Copyright, Designs and Patents Act 1988.

This is a work of fiction.

All characters, locations and events in this publication are fictitious and any resemblance to real persons, living or dead, or true events is purely coincidental.

Cover design by Genevieve Alice May Tomkins.

The original painting 'A Rainbow Fluttered By,' used in the cover design was painted by Genevieve Alice May Tomkins (née Walshaw) © 2018.

Redemption

Acknowledgements

There are so many people to thank for their patience, inspiration, encouragement and support in recent months. My wonderful family put up with a great deal, keeping me well supplied with tea, biscuits, hugs and healthy doses of sanity on a regular basis. Thanks for patiently stepping around all the wet canvases I leave lying around the house and politely ignoring me as I scribble madly in notebooks at random points in time.

To my wonderful Editor, PR guru and friend Liz Gordon of Brilliant Fish PR I have to say a huge thank you for your tactful and wise guidance.

Thank you again to Gill Donnell for being so inspirational and to Bev Hepting for teaching me everything I needed to know with regard to speaking out about my story. You are both absolute stars!

I must also give a huge shout out for my fellow synchronised swimmers from the Bransgore Evening WI. It was so much fun being part of a team made up of such inspirational ladies.

Finally let me send massive hugs and my unending gratitude to everyone who has played a part, big and small, in the creation of this final part of the trilogy from The House That Sat Down. I couldn't have done it without you.

Books by Alice May:

The House that Sat Down Trilogy

Book 1
Accidental Damage – *Tales from the house that sat down.*

Book 2
Restoration – *More tales from the house that sat down.*

Book 3
Redemption – *Moving on from the house that sat down.*

Redemption

For

Patricia Naomi Walshaw
Grandmother, Artist and Inspiration

*Thank you for giving a six-year old child a dream.
Who knew it would take me forty years to realise it?*

Yet here I am!

Contents

Part 1

    Preamble
    Chapter 1. Volunteer
    Chapter 2. Subconscious
    Chapter 3. Perception
    Chapter 4. Concatenation

Part 2

    Chapter 5. Momentous
    Chapter 6. Inquisition
    Chapter 7. Modification
    Chapter 8. Inducement
    Chapter 9. Adaptation

Part 3

    Chapter 10. Transmutation
    Chapter 11. Conversion
    Chapter 12. Germination
    Chapter 13. Evolution

Part 4

    Chapter 14. Resilience
    Chapter 15. Nascent
    Chapter 16. Incubation
    Chapter 17. Stymie
    Chapter 18. Exposure

Part 5

    Chapter 19. Self-confidence
    Chapter 20. Incongruous
    Chapter 21. Unwonted
    Chapter 22. Recalcitrant
    Chapter 23. Consolidation

Redemption

Part 6

    Chapter 24. Potential
    Chapter 25. Prorogation
    Chapter 26. Skulduggery
    Chapter 27. Crepuscular
    Chapter 28. Coelescence
    Chapter 29. Exhilaration

Epilogue

Alice May

PART 1

"No matter how hard the past, you can always begin again."

Buddha

Alice May

Preamble

Definition: A quick word from the author to establish a time frame

Welcome back my dear friends. As you may remember, I hadn't ever intended to write more than the one book 'Accidental Damage'. However, in time, I began to realise that there was more to my story and so I wrote the sequel 'Restoration' and was convinced that this was the end of the story. No-one could be more surprised than I was to find myself thumping away at my keyboard for a third time. It would seem that there was yet more to my tale, as the house that sat down had a surprising legacy in store.

When you last heard from our heroine she seemed to be sorting herself out. She had enjoyed a successful solo art exhibition at a local gallery, having come to terms with the difficult decision to let the family home go. It is my intention to continue my tale in the past from that point as the family reluctantly attempts to sell their beautifully rebuilt cottage. Unfortunately, certain political shenanigans at the time have caused the market to stagnate and they haven't had much luck finding a buyer, but they are not letting that get them down.

However, I will also be telling you what is happening in the present, approximately 6 months after the art exhibition finished, because some interesting things are afoot right now. I shall attempt to weave the past and present time frames together so that we can arrive at a final conclusion. Our leading lady has been on an incredible journey, the direction of which she could not possibly have imagined the day she stood on her drive and watched the walls of her home and the pieces of her ordinary life fall apart.

But enough of such story spoilers for the moment. All will be revealed in time.

Right at this moment she is rolling around on the dusty old floorboards of the stage at the local village hall, wiggling her legs in the air in a most unseemly fashion. In front of an audience!

"Oh dear!" I hear you say. "That is most unlike her." You could be forgiven for asking yourself whether she has finally lost the plot.

Hmmm...quite possibly! What on earth has she got herself into this time?

It's a long story.

I'll let her start telling you all about it now.

1. Volunteer
Definition: To freely offer to take part in a task, or assist in the undertaking of an event

Let us kick this tale off in the present day...

I could not believe I was doing this! What on earth had possessed me? I was prancing around on stage. In full view of not only people I knew, but also quite a few that I didn't know! This was not normal; I simply don't do this sort of thing. Ever!

Let me give you the full picture just for the record, I was wearing a wetsuit (one of the 'shorty' variety), a luminous pink shower cap with white spots on it, goggles and I had a piece of tinsel tied round each of my ankles. It was fortunate that this was a man-free zone. I was not a pretty sight.

Just as I was beginning to think I had completely taken leave of my senses, the sound of laughter reached my ears. It would seem that the ladies in the audience were enjoying the show, which made me smile in spite of my reservations.

Please remind me, the next time I decide to volunteer for something, that I really should find out precisely what is entailed before signing on the dotted line. When a clipboard and pen had been shoved under my nose at the end of a Women's Institute meeting six weeks ago and I was asked if I would like to be in the Christmas show, all I thought was that it was nice to be asked to join in. I didn't like to say no. I thought that it might be quite fun to be in a little nativity play. While I have never really liked being the centre of attention, I don't like to be a spoilsport either. It's a tricky line to tread. As I scrawled my name on the list, I thought that perhaps I could be a silent shepherd lurking at the back of the stage disguised by a fake beard and a tea towel on my head. Or failing that, I was certain I would make a superlatively self-effacing sheep or perhaps some other variety of bashful barnyard beast. In my mind that would be perfect. I could take part without being too obvious.

Silly me! (Note to self: Always read the small print and never make assumptions, especially where the Women's Institute is concerned!)

About a week later, I turned up to the first rehearsal clutching a suitably stripy tea towel, to find myself part of a small but very glamorous group of ladies who had no intention of doing any form of 'traditional' Christmas entertainment. There was to be no nativity at all! No shy shepherd, no coy cow, not even a diffident donkey. That would be far too boring. I don't know whose bright idea it was (well I do really, though I am naming no names) but several weeks of arduous rehearsals later, here we were at the Christmas Party doing a synchronised swimming routine.

On stage!

Minus a swimming pool!

I know! Totally mad!!

In fact, if I'm honest, we were lacking a fair degree of synchronisation too but no one seemed to be too worried about that; if the chuckles, giggles and downright belly laughs from the audience were anything to go by.

Redemption

There is one thing I've learned recently and it is that the ladies of the WI don't let minor difficulties get in their way. I have yet to meet a more spirited bunch of women. These zany females are a very determined lot! Much could be learned from them.

With a sheet of blue plastic draped over a rope, stretched across the lower third of the stage to indicate the water, our 'swimming' routine was taking place behind it, with either our upper half on display or, alternatively, just our legs poking up whilst we lay on our backs out of sight. The middle section of the routine involved some rather tortuous floor positions in order to achieve the desired effect, but I am sure you can use your imagination so I won't go into any more detail other than to say think of a rather intense Pilates class and you will be halfway there. It was generating an awful lot of hilarity, from the ladies on stage as well as the audience, which was obviously the point. Contrary to what I had expected, I was actually quite enjoying myself. Who knew making a fool of oneself in public would be so much fun?

Eventually our time in the spotlight came to a close as the music, the Blue Danube, ended and each swimmer did a flourishing 'dive' into (i.e. behind) the plastic water - not an easy feat when you consider our average age and the advanced arthritis afflicting some of our 'athletes'. We all landed in a somewhat undignified, tangled heap on the floor behind the plastic sheet and hurriedly sorted ourselves out to lie in a row on our tummies, chins propped up on our palms, facing the audience as the 'water' came down and loud applause rang out.

Alice May

What followed was quite a lot of indelicate scrambling as we got to our feet. In our defence, it's really not very easy to move around in a wetsuit on dry land, as they are rather restrictive. I liked to think that I had a small advantage over the others, having had had plenty of practice moving about in thick layers of clothing when we were living the garden the year before last, after the house fell down, but it probably wasn't true. Nevertheless, we eventually managed to form a ragged line and took a bow to what was a standing ovation, before those talented ladies who were nominated as Artistic Director, Choreographer, and Musical Director stepped forward to take a well-deserved additional bow.

There was a rather hurriedly cobbled together encore - we hadn't expected to be asked to do one and therefore hadn't choreographed one, so it was a bit random. Eventually, we were relieved to see the curtain come down for the final time. There are only so many times you can throw yourselves to the floor in a pretend 'dive' in one evening and get away with it. I had my suspicions that we were all going to be sporting some rather impressive bruises the next day.

Hastily stripping off sweaty wetsuits behind the curtains on stage with the rest of the troupe and slipping into something a bit more glam for the rest of the party, it was soon time to join everyone out in the main hall. After our exertions, we were definitely all set to tuck into a large glass of wine and some of the gorgeous gourmet delights displayed on groaning tables. I was surprised how quickly the time flew by because it wasn't long before it was time to help clear away, then scoop up my wetsuit and scuttle outside in a merry festive haze of goodbye hugs to find Beloved Husband waiting in the car outside ready to give me a lift home.

Redemption

***

I won't lie to you, getting up the next morning was a bit of a struggle. The combination of bruises and a few strained muscles from the 'swimming' routine, coupled with a bit of a muzzy head from the wine (I only had 2 glasses and they were small ones, honest!) plus the cold, dark December mornings all made me consider giving up on the idea of getting up at all. If only I could simply choose to hibernate for the rest of the winter. Wouldn't that be nice?

Beloved Husband was already up and gone. Facing a long early morning commute to his first meeting of the day, he had battled his way out from under the duvet at 6am with all the finesse of a very rumpled, grumpy lion. I valiantly ignored his growling about how unfair it was that he had to get up so early, and the fact that he insisted on putting the light on so that he could make sure he was wearing matching socks. Personally, I always think wearing odd socks is much easier and far more interesting but he cannot bring himself to do it.

However, when he started muttering that his shirt hadn't been ironed, I simply pulled the duvet over my head and tuned him out completely. He is nearly fifty years old and should know by now that there is no such thing as an ironing fairy. Not in this house anyway. If he wants something ironed he should do it himself, or give me three weeks advanced notice. Even then there'd be no guarantee I'd actually do it, unless he bribes me of course. I wasn't too worried about his griping though because I knew he'd cheer up soon enough. He's usually a fairly happy chap. He just doesn't do mornings terribly well. Or ironing, for that matter, although I have wondered if, like the washing up, he does it deliberately badly so that some unsuspecting female (i.e. me) will step in and say "Oh for goodness sake, you're making a right pig's ear of that, let me do it." Happily, I am wise to such tactics which is just as well because there are only the four of us at home now; three fellas and me. I could be ironing and washing up all day if I fell for such obvious ploys. But enough of such mundane matters!

He eventually stomped off down the stairs to ransack the kitchen before leaving the house, so I switched the light back off and I snuggled down to enjoy an extra half an hour in my lovely, warm bed. One of the things I really appreciated these days was my bed. Having had to go without it for so long after the house collapsed, I cannot tell you how much I cherished the simple act of going to bed every evening, falling asleep in warm, safe comfort and then waking up the next morning fully rested and ready to take on the hectic pace of daily life in this mad house.

I was very tempted to stay right where I was that morning, regardless of the fact that it was a Wednesday and I had the school run to do, which would be followed by a lengthy to-do list including both a shift at work and then lots of house-related tasks. For just a little while I pretended that I could 'accidentally' sleep in and stay in my cosy nest indefinitely.

As if it could ever be that simple.

Only a blink of an eye later and our youngest Barbarian (a term of endearment for our children), we call him Small, knocked noisily on the bedroom door before poking his head around it and rudely interrupting my daydream.

"Mum!' He whispered loudly, "Are you awake?"

Redemption

There was a pause while I checked if I was willing to admit that I was awake.

"No!" I answered eventually.

"Oh!" Sounding a bit confused by my answer, he obviously decided that I was joking and pushed the door open a bit more so he could slip in to the room, before sitting heavily on the side of the bed next to me and continuing, "I brought you a cup of tea."

Now that did get my attention. He never makes me tea. Something must be up. Rubbing my eyes briefly, I struggled into a more upright position, which is not easy when someone is sitting on top of the duvet next to you and effectively pinning you in place. Extricating enough of my upper self to be able to lean back against the headboard and switch the light back on, I quickly took hold of the wobbly cup of tea that was being waved in my general direction.

As I mentioned, we call our youngest Barbarian Small. It seemed appropriate at the time. Of course, ironically, he is now nearly twelve years old and is already taller than me, so it is a bit of a misnomer. Admittedly I am only 5 feet 2 inches in height, but he is genuinely quite tall for a boy his age.

"I didn't know you could make tea," I said, looking somewhat suspiciously into the cup.

"I can't," he admitted. "Quiet made it!"

"OK!" I said, wondering what his big brother was up to. I never get given tea in bed, not even on my birthday. I didn't have long to ponder this as the sound of a rather heavy tread came up the stairs. A moment later the bedroom door crashed right back on its hinges and Quiet appeared, brandishing a plate of toast and Marmite. As you can probably work out from my older son's name, just as Small isn't actually small any more, Quiet can no longer be described as being even remotely quiet. He has grown so much in recent months that I don't think he's remotely adjusted to his new proportions; hence he keeps accidentally bashing into things. He's not enormous, just quite a bit bigger than he used to be, and as a result significantly noisier.

Leaning over, he shoved the plate of toast under my nose and asked, "How was the show?"

Goodness me; tea, toast and polite conversation, all before 7.05 in the morning! I looked at the alarm clock to check. He was remarkably awake, organised and cheerful. Something was definitely afoot.

"Fine, thank you," I replied, trying to keep suspicion from colouring my tone.

"Good." He gave me a quick grin, shoved his shoulder away from the door frame and disappeared. As I listened to his heavy tread thumping back down the stairs, I looked at Small.

"That's strange," I said casually, "what's he up to?"

"Dunno," came the unhelpful reply from my youngest child, who then nodded at me gravely before levering himself off the bed and stomping after his brother.

Redemption

I sighed. This was going to require some investigation but, in the meantime, I planned to enjoy the unexpected treat of tea and toast in bed for five minutes. As I sat back with my surprise breakfast, I recalled the fun of the evening before. It had gone really rather well considering my previous experiences with Christmas shows.

The village hall had had been the location of a number of productions over the years, some more memorable than others. I could vividly recall the girls' first nativity in which they both appeared as angels sporting tinsel halos on springs attached to their heads via a nineteen-eighty's 'deely-bopper' style hairband arrangement. Unfortunately, mid-performance, Chaos discovered that if she nodded her head firmly enough she could get her halo to bounce down from above her head to gently bash her nose and found this most entertaining. Distracted from the song that the Archangel Gabriel and his gang were supposed to be singing at that point, she did this repeatedly to growing sniggers from the audience, while I watched helplessly with mounting mortification.

Unaware that all eyes were on her, Chaos then decided to demonstrate her newfound skill to Logic who was standing next to her. Sadly, in her enthusiasm, she misjudged the distance between them and accidentally head-butted her poor sister instead. Surprised by this unprovoked attack, Logic was thrown off balance and staggered backwards with her arms outstretched to try to stop falling off the stage. Unfortunately, she didn't achieve this objective and, as my younger daughter tumbled, she managed to haul the entire heavenly host with her in a flurry of white cotton smocks with rustling tinsel trims. It was certainly a very dramatic finale to the whole production, if not quite that which had been rehearsed. The entire audience leapt to their feet as one body, but obviously not to applaud. Instead we all began extracting small children from the jumbled pile, assured ourselves that there were no bones broken and then calmed them all down with hugs and kisses followed by squash and biscuits.

It was with some trepidation, therefore, that I attended the nativity at the same hall a year later, when Quiet had been cast as King Number One. He had the important job of delivering gold to the Holy Infant. In his defence, I suspect that there had probably been one too many dress rehearsals prior to the big event because my normally very reticent older son staged an unexpected rebellion. He adamantly refused to go on stage, loudly declaring that he was not going to walk to Bethlehem *again* because he'd been there yesterday, and the day before, and he was tired. Apparently, all the other kings agreed with him.

When I tentatively approached our wonderful village pre-school with my fourth child a few years later, I was very surprised that they even let me through the door. I am quite sure that a more delightfully calm and forgiving group of pre-school teachers could not be found anywhere else on this planet because they welcomed him with open arms, in spite of his unfortunate family connections. Luckily, the fourth time proved to be the charm as Small's pre-school Christmas show, a non-religious yet culturally diverse tale about a singing spaceman with a confusing collection of colourful crustacean cronies, passed without a hitch.

Phew! Practice makes perfect!

Redemption

Eventually, having crunched my way through my toast and finished my tea, I had to stop reminiscing about plays gone past and actually get sorted for the day ahead. It was time to start that lengthy to-do list I mentioned, all the while also trying to figure out my older Barbarian boy's bizarre behaviour.

2. Subconscious

Definition: the part of the mind that a person is not fully aware of but which can unobtrusively guide their actions, responses and emotions.

*Staying with the **present** for the time being....*

Arriving back at the house, none the wiser, at about midday after ticking several jobs off my to-do list, I had a couple of hours to spare before I was going to have to launch myself into the whole after school chauffeuring routine. I quickly fed the washing machine and switched on the kettle, when the phone rang. I picked up the handset to hear my mother's lively tones echoing down a rather crackly line.

"Oh, I am so glad I caught you. I'll be quick. I know you're busy. Do you remember my friend from bridge? The one I told you about, her sister's husband's brother is on the committee for the local literary and creative arts society."

I absently wondered where she was going with this information, as I tucked the phone under my chin so I could still hear her, and opened the fridge in order to see if Quiet had left any milk for my cup of tea. My older son's breakfast these days seemed to consist of a deep serving bowl filled with the white stuff plus almost an entire box of whatever random cereal he could find in the cupboard swimming in it. I assumed that it had something to do with calcium and all that growing he was doing. He had also developed a habit of consuming a whole pint glass full of yet more milk at random points during the day, which meant that keeping the supply level equal with the demand was proving to be quite a challenge. It didn't make any difference that we were living

Redemption

in the deepest darkest countryside, surrounded by herds of dairy cows. Getting him to hop over the fence into the nearest field with a clean bucket was, unfortunately, not an option; I still had to go to a supermarket to buy milk by the shedload like everyone else.

I pounced on a suspiciously empty looking four-pint plastic bottle hopefully, having realised fairly recently that, in order to deal with his guilt at not bothering to cross the room to put the empty bottle in the recycling bin, Quiet had taken to leaving small dregs in the base. This was probably so that he could claim there was still some left, which in his mind completely justified the typically lazy teenage act of putting an empty container back in the fridge.

While upending the carton over my mug and watching the smallest smidgen of remaining milk turn my black tea into an indiscriminately murky, slightly-less-black version, a sixth sense made me tune back into what my mother was saying.

"So anyway, I told her you'd do it?"

Alarm bells rang immediately. I'd obviously missed something important, what on earth was my mother up to now?

"I'm sorry, what did you tell her I'd do?"

"Go to the literary and creative arts society and give a forty-five minute presentation."

"What?" My world momentarily tipped on its axis and it suddenly became very difficult to breathe as advanced panic set in. "I can't do that!"

"Don't be silly darling, of course you can!" continued my mother blithely. "You gave a lovely presentation at your exhibition last May."

"Mother, that hardly counts!" I exclaimed, "I stood up for about ten minutes and waffled on about a few paintings. I shook like a leaf and probably bored everyone senseless. I can't even remember what I said. It was awful!"

"Nonsense!" she countermanded briskly. "You did very well. This would be the same sort of thing, only it's a bit longer. They'll probably want to ask lots of questions."

"Forty-five minutes is quite a bit longer!" I exclaimed faintly, feeling nauseous. "What on earth would I say?" But my mother didn't seem to register my concern and carried on regardless.

"Oh well, that's easy darling," she said breezily. "You tell them your story, show them some paintings and then talk about writing your book."

"My book!"

It was true, I had written a book. (I know there's a fair chance that you know this because if you are reading this one then you've probably read the first one, and probably the second one too, but feel free to pretend you haven't if it helps.)

"It's not a real book," I wailed. It was only a small self-published novel and nothing to be taken too seriously. To be frank, I had rather surprised myself by writing it in the first place and now that I had, I didn't really know what to do with it, so I was quite happily ignoring its existence.

"It is real!" she countered firmly. "I've read it. It's funny, and the society members will love hearing from an author. Your road to publication, that sort of thing."

"But it's only self-published."

"What's that got to do with anything? It makes it more interesting if you ask me. What about that fifty shadows woman? She was self-published!"

"You really can't compare my book with Fifty Shades of Grey mum." I said wryly. "There is absolutely no similarity whatsoever."

"And thank goodness for that, I wouldn't have posted a copy of your book off to my cousin's wife if there was! But that's not the point. Self-publishing is the up and coming thing for authors these days." My mother was probably the only person in the world who had actually bought a copy of my book.

"I seriously don't think I can do this," I sighed.

"You'll be fine. The society members are all amateur creative persons themselves, just like you, and they'll be so interested in how you've gone about it all. Just go along and have a little chat with them. It'll be easy. Some of them might even buy the book, if you take some copies with you, and perhaps a painting or two. You'll have a lovely time."

Alice May

Typically biased in my favour, as parents often are towards their offspring, my mother thinks I can do anything, which is wonderfully supportive of course but not always terribly accurate. Had she not noticed that I had spent the last 46 years actively avoiding public speaking in any form? (Apart from a little divergence from that policy at my solo exhibition last year, which, while it hadn't been quite as bad as all that, wasn't an experience I was keen to repeat.) All through school I had managed to never stand up in front of anyone and say anything. It was quite an achievement, one that had taken careful planning and forethought and I didn't intend to change things now.

There was a moment or two of silence as I went into a little mental bubble of anxiety. I took a couple of deep, slow breaths to steady myself and eventually my mother continued, "Well, you have a little think about it and let me know. I have to go now, darling, I've got my tap class and then your dad and I are meeting up with friends from the French Twinning Association for coffee. I'll call you tomorrow. Bye!" With that breezy farewell she was gone. Off to the myriad social engagements my parents got up to now they were retired.

I slumped onto one of the stools by the breakfast bar, put the handset down on the surface before me and stared unseeing into the depths of my dark teacup. What was she thinking? There was no way I could ever do any real public speaking.

Satisfied that this was the end of the matter, I was quite surprised to hear a defiant little voice from the depths of my subconscious stating quite clearly and very seriously, "It's not a bad idea"

Redemption

"It is a terrible idea," I countered in surprise. "I really can't do it." I said this very firmly indeed, just to make sure I understood myself.

"Why?" My inner voice piped up again to demand defiantly.

"I don't do public speaking, ever!" I said with conviction.

"You didn't think you'd write a book either," the voice inside replied. I ought to clarify here that I wasn't actually hearing things; honestly! It was just that the words seemed to spring into my head unbidden from nowhere.

"I haven't written a book." I told myself.

"Errr, I beg to differ..." (How come my inner voice sounded like a sarcastic teenager?)

"Oh, you know what I mean. Not really. I'm not a proper author."

"Authors write books, you've written a book..."

"It's not the same thing," I said, wondering why on earth I was arguing with myself.

"Lots of people would like to write a book, not many actually do it. You've done it. Give yourself some credit for once. Things change," reasoned my subconscious earnestly. "You've changed!"

Alice May

'Yes!' I mentally muttered, very quietly (in case I heard myself), 'I am clearly now such a total nut case that I am having a row with myself!'

I stood up abruptly.

"I'm very busy!" I said firmly, out loud again this time. "So, stop going on about it, I've got things to do." I think it was Buddha who said: 'Rule your mind or it will rule you.' Rather apt I felt, given the circumstances! Squashing down any further subconscious responses very resolutely indeed, I bustled around getting my hessian carrier bags out so I could go and do a quick smash and grab at the local supermarket to stock up on milk and other sundries.

I hastily went through my 'leaving the house' checklist which involves a quick glance in every room to make sure the kids (or the husband) haven't left anything electronic on that might blow up or burn the place down while I'm out. Yes, I am still paranoid. Then I switched off all the lights (because teenagers are physically incapable of doing that, hence every single light in the house was on) and locked both the back and front doors. (No-one else ever seems to do that around here either.) Just to be on the safe side, I stuck a spare door key behind the skull and crossbones badge on the brim of Skelly's tri-corn hat as I passed him on my way to the car. The family skeleton was lounging lazily on a large, upturned, wooden bucket by the fence, doing an excellent impression of an extra from the Pirates of the Caribbean film. One could almost expect Captain Jack Sparrow to rock up and sit next to him any minute.

Now that Quiet was in the sixth form and some of his friends had passed their driving tests, he had a habit of hitching a lift

Redemption

home from school early with one of them, but he never remembered to take his door key with him and then grumped when he couldn't get in. I had taken to hiding a spare key for him so that when he rang me up and grumbled about being locked out, I could present him with a solution that wouldn't cause me any undue inconvenience. I reasoned that not many burglars would be brave enough to frisk a skeleton for a spare key, especially one armed with such a realistic looking plastic sabre and two flintlock pistols, so in my mind it was a fairly secure system.

Finally, I settled myself comfortably in Daisy, my little purple car, and we were off, satisfied that there was a fairly good chance the house might still be standing on our return. (Lightening? Twice? It happens!)

As I negotiated the ford further down the road, I started to wonder what had made me write a book in the first place. I had never had any ambitions to be an author and yet when it started, I had been powerless to resist. It was as if some force had taken over and consumed me completely until the story was told. Perhaps that's why I didn't feel it was real.

Nevertheless, while I didn't know why, I did know when. It had all started about six months earlier when we had finally accepted that we needed to put our home on the market, an act that was to have some very unexpected consequences indeed.

3. Perception
Definition: The way in which something might be interpreted or judged.

*Back in the **past**, approximately six months earlier, soon after the house was put up for sale*

"This kitchen is just no good at all," the rather haughty woman declared in a somewhat nasal tone. "I run a professional catering business. I give classes from home. I would need to have large groups watching me demonstrate."

Mentally rolling my eyes and thinking 'We've got a right one here!' I started to sidle slowly towards the door, intent on extricating myself from the general conversation as soon as possible.

It was the end of August and our beautiful cottage had been on the market for nearly two months. Rebuilding our home, after it had collapsed unexpectedly, had cost us dearly in both emotional and financial terms, hence we were left in possession of a scarily big mortgage; so big in fact that we'd given it a name. We'd christened our mortgage Mortimer, in an attempt to make him seem more friendly and approachable. That tactic hadn't worked particularly well, so immediately after my art exhibition we had got stuck in to do all the things you are supposed to do when putting your house up for sale, with the intention of significantly reducing Mortimer as soon as possible. We've seen the daytime TV shows like The House Doctor and Escape to the Country. It's not rocket science. Everyone knows you consider your kerb appeal, slap a bit of fresh paint around, get a neutral carpet

Redemption

and de-clutter till the cows come home before sitting back and waiting for an acceptable offer.

Let's look at those elements in more detail, shall we? There was no doubt that we'd been forcibly 'decluttered' when the house fell down, so that was not really an issue. If anything, we didn't have enough junk around the place. The house looked a bit too sparse, in an obsessively minimalist way. We were missing a lot of essentials, especially on the furniture front, so I had used my imagination and created several small occasional tables from cardboard boxes disguised with all-encompassing tablecloths draped over them. It was important to remember which items were counterfeit and not to accidentally put anything heavy on them or you'd get predictable and often messy results.

As for fresh paint, there was plenty of that already on the brand new walls; it was barely dry from the rebuild. Similarly, the carpets, a lovely pale biscuit colour, had only just gone down.

I left the kerb appeal side of things to my gardening and power tool obsessed husband. (There is no point having a dog and then barking yourself now, is there?) He had happily hacked the exponential summer growth from the front hedges and then cheerfully chopped the overgrown vegetation at the roadside verge into submission as well, before turning his hand to planting up a profusion of pelargoniums in pots. There was even an abundance of flowery climbers flourishing up the fence by the garage as well.

All I had to do after that was keep the place looking tidy, which is no mean feat when you share living space with two 'back for the summer vacation' students, three untidy fellas and a six-foot skeleton with a fancy dress fetish and a penchant for lurking in unexpected locations. It meant that nearly all my free time was spent either trying to keep on top of the housework myself or chivvying the other residents to do their fair share (which actually took far longer and was much less effective than doing everything myself, but that's not the point). Neither featured as one of my favourite occupations by any stretch of the imagination, but you really can't leave knickers drying in the conservatory on racks when any old Tom, Dick or Harriet might pop by at a moment's notice to eye up your square footage with a view to making a potential property purchase offer, can you? It simply didn't fit with the whole 'luxury lifestyle image' that we were trying to promote in order to get a decent sale price. Shame that really but there you go. Needs must!

In fact, I was exhausted after a high-speed, last minute tidy up this morning for the snooty woman currently criticising my kitchen, and I was in no mood to try and placate her or point out the many positive attributes of the room. I edged towards the door leaving our extremely patient estate agent valiantly commenting, in a gently persuasive tone, that it was a touch unfair to expect to find a professional kitchen in what was a purely domestic property. As soon as I was around the corner and out of sight I fled to my studio while the estate agent waxed lyrical about beautifully generous proportions including not only the kitchen, but also a lounge area with an open fireplace and an adjoining conservatory section large enough to contain a table that seated 12 when fully extended.

Not a small room by any standards really, unless you are feeling particularly picky. And thank goodness for that! For

Redemption

nearly eighteen months the whole family had often spent all day together in that one room after the rest of the house had fallen down. We had frequently slept on the floor by the fire rather than spend another soggy night in a tent during the worst of the weather.

To be fair though, while our haughty house-viewer was being a touch overbearing with her comments about her catering business, she'd probably never been in such an awful situation and therefore not learned to see life in quite the way we did, and why should she? In many ways I was glad for her, because I wouldn't wish what had happened to us on anyone. Nevertheless, that didn't mean that I had to stick around to hear her pick holes in my property. That was why we had employed the lovely Patience and her other estate agent colleagues and they were very good at their jobs.

Once in the studio, I gave myself over to prepping canvases for future paintings. At that time, I was very 'into' creating textured bases onto which I would then paint ocean or plant images. The resultant uneven canvas surfaces gave the finished pieces much greater depth and they were really exciting to paint on, as I never quite knew how each one was going to turn out. Merrily slapping glue and layers of crumpled tissue paper onto several stretched canvases, I was getting into a right old sticky mess, when Patience eventually popped her head around the door.

"She's gone," she announced with a smile." It's safe to come out now. Shame on you for not having a professional kitchen!"

Alice May

"I know!" I replied, "Silly me! I should have realised she'd want one when we had the kitchen put in twelve years ago. Can I assume that she won't be putting in an offer then?"

"I think we can safely say that she's not interested, although I am not really sure where she'll find what she's looking for. Especially when you consider her budget," Patience grimaced and rolled her eyes. "It's probably a bit too remote here for her anyway. We will find you a buyer, I promise, it's just going to take some time. This is rather a unique property."

I nodded thoughtfully. "Yes, I can see that it wouldn't be everyone's cup of tea, living this far out of town, but we love it. It's so peaceful."

If it weren't for Mortimer we wouldn't dream of selling up, but unfortunately it wasn't that straightforward. It also wasn't proving easy to find a buyer because although the house was now beautifully restored and in perfect structural and general working order, the current housing market was not terribly buoyant and there were very few legitimate buyers in our particular price bracket. There was no point dropping the price because that wouldn't solve our financial situation, so we were effectively between a rock and a hard place and simply had to tighten our belts and stick it out.

Patience made as if to leave, but then turned back with what I had learned in recent weeks was her 'tactful' expression. I paused, gluey brush in hand, "You look like you have a suggestion."

She smiled and nodded, "Two suggestions, actually."

Redemption

"Go on." I braced myself, placing my brush down and folding my arms in a subconsciously defensive gesture.

She cast an eye around my studio. "The rest of the house is beautifully presented, but this room isn't particularly doing you any favours right now."

I followed her gaze. It was a bit cluttered, I supposed. I often didn't bother to put my paints away because it just wasted precious painting time getting them out again. There were also several unfinished wet paintings on the go, one on the easel, a small one on the desk by the window and one propped up on the mantelpiece. Finally, the textured canvases I was working on, although small, were lined up on layers of newspaper on the floor surrounded by tissue paper and pots of PVA glue.

OK, I didn't like it but I had to concede that she had a point! Don't get me wrong though, the rest of the house was beautifully tidy. I'd spent hours vacuuming carpets and polishing stuff over the last few weeks, even though all I really wanted to do was get on with finishing the painting commissions I'd recently taken on.

"So, you're suggesting I tidy it up a bit."

She nodded sympathetically, "Quite a bit. Just in here, everywhere else in the house is fine."

"OK!" I agreed.

She didn't continue.

"And the second thing?" I prompted.

"Well," she paused.

"Go on," I encouraged. If there was something that would better our chances of achieving a sale then I needed to know what it was.

She sighed, "It's your skeleton….."

"Oh, hell!" I said, "I thought I'd hidden him. Where is he this time?"

"At the moment he's in the utility room, behind the door, on a hook hanging by the neck with what looks like a school tie….?"

That's definitely not where I left him, and the school tie really ought to be around someone else's neck right at that moment, otherwise he'd get a detention!

Patience continued carefully, "As I said, I don't think this lady was going to buy anyway, but finding the skeleton….well…."

"It put the final nail in the coffin, right?"

She smiled at my unintentional pun and nodded.

"You do know he's not real, don't you?" My fingers instinctively crossed behind my back as I asked this because, in truth, I had no idea if he was or not.

"Oh yes, but he is remarkably realistic and unfortunately I do think some people might be finding him a touch off-putting."

Redemption

"Some people have no sense of humour!" I muttered.

Skelly was now, very definitely, part of the family after arriving for a Halloween party during the time that we lived in the garden, and then never leaving. His antics at the time had cheered us all up immensely during a very dark period, but I could see what she meant. We couldn't expect normal people to 'get' him particularly.

"Don't worry," I said, "I'll sort it out."

After Patience had left (no doubt to be perfectly patient at another property where I bet they hadn't got a mobile skeleton problem), I sat and stared at my canvases for quite some time. I'd rather gone off the idea of painting now. Pealing layers of dried PVA glue off my fingers, I decided that my lovely estate agent was probably right. It was going to be a painful process but this studio needed sorting out, and sooner rather than later.

Tidying up never features at the top of my list of 'favourite things to do'. It always makes me grumpy and is, therefore, usually best avoided. My reasoning follows the logic that the mess will still be there tomorrow, whereas the urge to paint might not be. (Unless my mother or my mother-in-law plan to visit of course, in which case everything needs to be tidied up immediately.) In fact, clearing up in the grand scheme of things generally doesn't appear on my 'to do' list at all, but that doesn't mean it doesn't need doing of course. Since the house had been on the market there had been far too much tidying up going on, in my opinion.

I've probably given you the impression that I'm slovenly, but that isn't the case, honestly. The house is usually reasonably neat, as I tend to keep on top of things as I go along, but it doesn't generally have the sort of polish required for a viewing in the natural course of our day-to-day lives as a family. There are too many people actually trying to get on with the business of living here for it to ever be a typical show home.

However, Patience was right, a bit more effort was definitely required in my studio and before I attempted to solve the Skelly situation, I reluctantly concentrated my efforts on tackling my cluttered creative space.

Several hours later I was exhausted. It wasn't a fun job by any stretch of the imagination, but I had to do what I could to improve our chances of getting a buyer. The sad thing was that this was going to mean some fairly drastic changes in my usual method of operation. I was going to have to restrict my painting schedule significantly in order to keep control of the state that this room got into. It wasn't something I was looking forward to. My whole ethos with art was to relax and enjoy it, to let go of constraints, forget the rules and just let colour and creativity flow. However, under current circumstances, that was now a luxury I couldn't afford.

Nevertheless, I had carefully collected up and sorted my profusion of painting paraphernalia into a number of neatly compartmented drawers and boxes. No longer were the acrylics, oils and watercolour tubes all tumbled together in a happy, haphazard heap, but regimented in strictly separate sections. Brushes, palette knives, rollers and rulers were organised into tidy rows of jolly jam jars sitting on systematically sorted shelves stuffed with outsized tubs of glue, natural sponges, and rolls of tissue paper, cellophane

Redemption

and bubble wrap. Sizeable sheets of mount board were stacked in ship-shape fashion behind the filing cabinet and pencils, charcoal, rulers and rubbers marched in smart straight lines in the top drawer of my desk by the window.

All of the finished canvases had been removed and stacked in one of the sheds and my easel had been dismantled and tucked behind the door out of sight.

The result was a light, bright, tidy room that looked very appealing. All my hard work had brought about pretty impressive results, but it made me feel sad. I wasn't sure I was ever going to be the type of person who was able to paint tidily and I had a worrying feeling that this was going to be a bit of a problem. However, if it meant that we sold the house then it would be worth it. I could always paint afterwards, assuming we found a house that was big enough.

Eventually I ran out of things to sort out in the studio and tiredly closed the door before heading into my 'unprofessional' kitchen in search of a sustaining snack, making a mental note to tackle the Skelly issue before the next viewing.

4. Concatenation

Definition: a whole series of things that have a connection. (I promise!)

*Staying with the situation in the **past**...*

A week or so after the big studio tidy up, at the beginning of September, I stood in a tiny, airless corridor surrounded by boxes of random stuff belonging to my younger daughter, Logic. Both the boxes and I were enveloped in the slightly stale aroma of 'eau de mildew' mixed with institutional bulk-buy bleach and, as such, I was trying hard not to need to breathe. The smell and the squeaky linoleum beneath my feet transported me instantaneously back to my long-forgotten arrival at university as a student, (more than 28 years ago, but who's counting?) and I noted with interest that halls of residence hadn't really changed all that much in the intervening period.

For various reasons I had found myself studying science at university when all I had really wanted to do was go to art college, having been inspired as a young child by my grandmother who was a very talented, amateur artist. But life doesn't generally work out the way we hope it will when we are six, does it? At the age of eighteen I had found myself studying for a 'proper' qualification instead. It was a sensible decision, made for all sorts of practical reasons and while I didn't regret it, a really tiny piece of me couldn't help lamenting a lost opportunity to follow that childhood dream.

A reminiscent sigh rolled down my spine, but I reminded myself that my role here today was that of 'dutifully supportive mother returning one of two student daughters

Redemption

to university for the second year'. As such, my opinion on the standard of her accommodation was irrelevant and I was only permitting myself to say bright and positive things like "How lovely!" "Isn't this exciting?" and "You are so lucky/clever/brilliant," interchanging the adjective as appropriate.

Now was not the time to start saying anything along the lines of: "Are you seriously planning to live here?" or "What on earth were you thinking when you signed the tenancy agreement for this dive?"

To be honest, it wasn't actually that bad as student accommodation goes. I'd seen much worse. Only last week I had moved my older daughter, Chaos, into a house for the start of her third year. Having been obsessed with wanting to see full structural surveys for the student house she had lived in last year, Chaos contrarily now seemed to be defiantly tempting fate with her latest rental property choice, as it appeared to have even less stability than the proverbial house of cards. I couldn't help but admire her blasé attitude.

Sadly, none of the family had got away with the whole 'whoops, the house has fallen down and we're homeless, let's go and live in a tent in the garden' experience scot-free. There had been a massive emotional price to pay after our cob cottage had collapsed. Yet while I would like to think that the nightmare of that time might eventually start to fade from her mind, I felt that Chaos' choice of accommodation was an act of deliberately brave rebellion; an open dare to the fates not to mess with her again.

Alice May

Her latest student house, on close inspection the previous week, gave all the appearance of being held together in places with little more than a combination of string, duct tape and a few half-hearted prayers. I was pretty certain that her cramped Victorian terrace dwelling was still standing only because the significantly better maintained houses on either side of it were holding it up. Neither Chaos nor her four house mates seemed to have noticed the huge crater in the kitchen floor, the hole in the back door covered with a dog-eared bit of old cardboard and sticky tape, or the missing third tread on the staircase. (I am not going to comment on the state of the bathroom!) But it didn't matter. They were happy and that was the most important thing. I reassured myself that in spite of all evidence to the contrary, it must have passed the necessary safety checks that are currently in force, as it was definitely on the university-approved housing list.

I checked.

Three times!

Now, I do appreciate that, given our recent history, I have a habit of overreacting and as a result I forced myself to take the view that if the state of the place didn't bother the students then why should it bother me? Contracts were already signed for the year and there was nowhere else available, so there was nothing I could do about it anyway.

Therefore, in view of her sister's extreme choice, it could be said that Logic's second year residential flat was quite reasonable, in spite of the creeping mould and a dodgy window (it doesn't quite close properly so there is a permanent draft which might prove an issue mid-winter but

Redemption

let's not borrow trouble). It was right in the city centre, so near countless bars and nightclubs which are inevitably essential for student life, and yet still only a short walk to campus. It was also quite economically priced she assured me.

Speaking of finances, let's not forget my other parental role on this day, which was to produce my credit card to solve any minor teething issues, such as forgotten duvet cases or essential kitchen equipment by purchasing replacements at the nearest department store.

Logic, energised by the prospect of the start of her second year of extra hard maths, (I know, she's crazy, but someone has to do it!) popped her head out of her new room with a bright smile on her face. "Won't be long, now just need to get organised, then I'll find the kettle and make us a brew," she said and, grabbing one of the boxes off the pile, disappeared again.

I wasn't really needed to guard her possessions in the corridor, but there was not enough space in her room for the two of us at the same time. I was beginning to wonder how she was going to get all her belongings in through the door, let alone put them away, but that was definitely her problem, not mine. She's always liked jigsaws and she gave every appearance of enjoying this particular conundrum. Shifting my position slightly so that I could peer into the somewhat bijou space that was to be her home for the next forty-two weeks, I studied the cramped room through the open doorway with interest. A three-quarter sized double bed took up ninety percent of the floor area, with a small wardrobe and desk unit running alongside it. A door next to the foot of the bed opened into a miniscule en-suite, a very grand term for what was effectively a toilet located within a shower cubicle. This arrangement effectively encouraged the student to multitask on matters of personal hygiene, as one could clean one's teeth whilst sitting on the loo and showering all at the same time, if one had a mind to. I supposed it would depend just how late the student was for lectures in the morning.

While most people might consider that this was a fairly impossible space to live and work in for any length of time, I couldn't help but be quite impressed by the design. It was very cleverly engineered, practical and efficient, as well as being significantly larger than the cupboard that Logic had lived in for almost a year after the house sat down and we moved lock, stock and barrel into Hattie the caravan. That whole entertaining experience had massively modified our expectations of general living facilities, and we tend to be grateful for what we have these days, rather than bother about what we don't.

Suddenly realising that the room looked rather empty, I wondered where Logic actually was. She had definitely gone into the room but wasn't visible now. They were very dinky dimensions for her to have successfully disappeared in. With some relief I spotted her feet, encased in a mismatching pair of funky socks (like mother, like daughter), sticking out from under the bed. Aha! Obviously, 'under bed storage' was the key solution for such a compact student life style, although I am sure you're not supposed to lounge around under there for long. I bet it never gets hoovered.

There was a muffled muttering followed by some energetic wriggling which made me question whether she needed some help extricating herself from the dark depths but,

Redemption

other than diving in and yanking hard on both legs, I wasn't sure how much assistance I could be. Instead I stayed at my post and watched as more of her came slowly into view until eventually her head popped out too. Shoving static, crackly hair out of her eyes, she looked over at me.

"So! It's a shame about your job, isn't it?" she said, bluntly.

Ah! I'd been wondering when that particular subject would come up. I looked at my feet for a second before answering.

"Yes, I suppose so," I replied vaguely.

The company that I had been working for, for the past twenty years, was in the process of changing hands and the new management structure would not include a role for me. I wasn't particularly devastated as it had never been a terribly inspiring job by any stretch of the imagination, merely something that I'd fallen into fairly early on in life. It was flexible, paid relatively well and fitted around our growing family's needs, and as a result I had stayed on way longer than I had ever imagined I would. Nevertheless, by the coming December, I would effectively be unemployed for the first time ever in my working life and it was requiring a bit of mental adjustment.

While I wasn't actually bothered about losing that particular job, it would inevitably add some pressure to our current financial situation (remember Mortimer?), so I was going to have to find another form of income fairly soon. However, there was to be a small severance pay out which would allow some breathing space before things got completely critical in the penny stakes. Selling the house would still help massively, but there was no sign of a buyer as yet. Either way, I was going to have to get another job of some description. The only problem was that I didn't really know what sort of job to go for. Feeling wrong-footed, I wasn't really in the mood to face the sort of Spanish Inquisition style interrogation that I suspected was about to be launched in my general direction.

In that moment I realised that my adored Barbarian offspring had definitely discussed my approaching unemployment situation at length, in private, and reached what they decided was the most appropriate course of action. No doubt Logic had been given the unenviable task of 'Sorting Mother Out'!

Unfortunately for Logic, I wasn't prepared to co-operate just then. I had been up since silly o'clock in order to crow-bar as much returning student-related detritus into Daisy as was humanly possible, and then I had spent nearly three hours trekking from the Hampshire border, across the wilds of Dorset, and Devon to reach the university. Poor Daisy had been so overloaded with the aforementioned student associated paraphernalia that making it to the top of some of the hills along the way had been extremely touch and go, even in first gear with my foot to the floor. Then, having arrived, we were faced with lugging all her junk up six flights of stairs (the lift was of course out of order – what a surprise!) to our current location on the top floor. All that had been accomplished without the aid of any breakfast; not even a cup of tea!

Whilst off caffeine for the most part, I usually need one cup of the 'proper' stuff to start the day. However, that morning I had been worrying about the lack of potential 'rest breaks' on route and so foolishly had left without my usual fix. As a

Redemption

result, I felt I was achieving a minor miracle just staying on my feet at that point, so the bright scholar before me would be wise not to push her luck. I wasn't as open to the experience of being organised by my offspring as I might have been under other circumstances. I really did not want to talk about my job situation, or the lack thereof, but Logic had that sensible expression on her face indicating the presence of a whole host of carefully collated questions. These were, no doubt, questions that I didn't currently have the answers to as I was still processing my change in circumstances and trying not to get stressed. Casting around for a distraction, I spotted what looked like the handle of the kettle peeking out of one of the boxes.

"Aha! There it is!" I exclaimed in relief, pouncing on it. "I'll just set this up in the communal kitchen for you, shall I?" I scooped up the box in the certain knowledge that if the kettle was in there then so would any tea and coffee making equipment; including mugs, teaspoons and probably even some milk in a little cool bag, if I know my daughter correctly. Logic is nothing if not…. well…. logical, hence her nickname. Backing away from the approaching cross-examination with indecent haste, I shoved the door that was helpfully marked 'Kitchen' with my comfortably padded rear end and disappeared inside with a fixed but polite 'I am ignoring you' expression on my face.

I knew I wouldn't get away with it for long but the words of one particular wise old Roman, Tacitus, were echoing around in my head. 'He who fights and runs away may turn to fight another day'. Hence, I beat a hasty retreat until such time as I felt a touch more resilient.

Anyway, enough of all this history for the moment; it is all connected to why I wrote my book, and I will get to the point soon, I promise, but let us return to the present for a bit, to see how things are developing.

PART 2

'Thinking, the talking of the soul with itself,'

Plato 424BC – 347BC

5. Momentous

Definition: **of significant importance, having a substantial effect on future events,**

Do please come forward in time with me once again to the present day, early January and our heroine heading for the supermarket...

I trundled along the wintery lanes in the general direction of civilisation and a milk supply, slowing for a small herd of horses, three super-fit looking joggers and a selection of dogs of indeterminate breed exercising their associated humans. Eventually, I turned Daisy into the car park of a reasonably-sized supermarket, all the while contemplating how the events that had unfolded six months earlier had led to the situation that I now found myself in. But that was when the little voice in my head started nagging me again.

"Your mother's right, you know."

"No, she isn't" I replied firmly.

"She is," the other me insisted. "You could put a fairly interesting presentation together. It might be fun."

"No, I couldn't, and no, it wouldn't be."

"Think about it."

"Be quiet!" I replied firmly, "I am trying to park."

Silence reigned as I reversed into a space and then headed into the shop armed with my hessian bags and a wonky

Redemption

trolley. Several packed aisles of produce later my subconscious tried again.

"On reflection, I don't think I want to be quiet," she piped up.

"For goodness sake," I hissed in frustration. Having loaded up with twelve pints of milk, I was then marching through the frozen food section looking for peas and oven chips to go with some sausages for supper.

"Give me one good reason why you can't do this," my inner voice was developing an increasingly belligerent tone.

"I can't, it'd be too embarrassing!" I muttered.

"Seriously? That's your reason?" replied my subconscious with a fair degree of disgust. "That's pretty pathetic, you know!"

"Oh, will you just go away!" I said forcefully, frowning fiercely at my internal self.

The old lady in the thick tweed overcoat who was peering short-sightedly at the frozen peas in the freezer cabinet, stiffened abruptly with an affronted huff, before scuttling off with surprising agility for one so elderly, whilst giving me nervous glances over her shoulder.

"Oh! Sorry, I don't mean you. I'm just talking to myself. Out loud," I said, watching her rapidly retreating rear in dismay.

"Was that what you meant by embarrassing?" piped up my subconscious sarcastically.

"Aagh!" I hissed in quiet frustration. "OK, I'll think about it! I promise. Now will you please leave me alone?"

"That's all I ask," said my subconscious smugly before fading out of my mind completely with an ominously final whisper that echoed around my mind, "I'll be back!"

"Great!" I said sarcastically to myself, grabbing a large bag of Birds Eye's best and shoving my trolley towards the tills, wondering if anyone else had to argue with such an opinionated subliminal self. How come I get saddled with such an outspoken and obstinate inner identity? Surely the very definition of the subconscious is that one is supposed to be blissfully unaware of it? Hmmm! I just might have to explain that to my bolshie alter ego one day soon. If she ever lets me get a word in sideways that is.

In spite of my embarrassing argument with myself in the supermarket, the rest of the afternoon passed relatively calmly, thank goodness, and I returned to my still-standing house (phew!) to find Quiet and a couple of his mates playing the PlayStation with Skelly in the lounge. It would seem that there was nothing more interesting happening on the Sixth Form timetable that afternoon.

Remembering my son's odd behaviour that morning, I watched him surreptitiously for a few minutes, but he seemed completely normal so I backed out of the room, closing the door on the way in order to dampen the noise of car races screeching away at a hundred plus miles per hour accompanied by cheers and other associated teenage boy banter. I unpacked the shopping hurriedly before diving into the freezer to locate those sausages I mentioned. My plan

Redemption

for the evening was to go to the WI meeting in the village whilst the boys and Beloved Husband were occupied at cricket training. They are always ravenous after training, so it made sense to cook their tea before I left so that they could microwave it quickly when they got home.

A few hours later, I was settling into my seat in the village hall next to my lovely neighbour as the meeting got underway. There is usually a very interesting presentation given at each WI meeting and, while I had not paid any attention to who was speaking this evening or what they planned to speak about, they are generally of a very high standard so I was looking forward to it.

Fifteen minutes into the meeting (and bang on time) after the general news and business had been discussed, the main door to the hall opened and a tall, confident, smartly dressed woman walked in, wheeling a little case behind her. She was welcomed warmly by the committee members and ushered to a table by a screen at the front of the room where she swiftly unzipped her case and drew out a laptop with a small projector attachment. These were assembled on the table at lightning quick speed and in moments she was smiling at her audience and ready to begin.

An impressively efficient start to what was, in truth, a very entertaining presentation. This lady was a particularly awesome individual who had spent her entire career supporting women in the working environment and encouraging them to reach their full potential. In fact, she had been awarded an MBE in recognition of her outstanding achievement and services to the community. Over the course of the next hour, she made us laugh with funny yet very motivational anecdotes about some of the gifted women that she had worked with over the years. She rounded off her talk by mentioning that she was keen to interview women with interesting stories and achievements for her podcast (I wasn't quite sure what a podcast was but nodded knowledgeably anyway), and would be delighted to hear recommendations or suggestions from any of the ladies in the audience.

Well! Talk about waving a red rag at a bull. My lovely neighbour immediately started elbowing me firmly in the ribs and in a stage whisper said, "You should tell her about your story!"

Uh oh!

"You know," she persisted, "about your house falling down. Tell her about writing your book."

If you remember, I mentioned earlier that I didn't expect anyone to read my book? Well, my neighbour was probably one of the few people on the planet who not only knew about it (she's met my mother), but had also read it (she's a very kind person). I smiled at her to acknowledge the compliment she was paying me by suggesting that I might be interesting enough to draw to the attention of the awesome lady speaker. Unfortunately, that wasn't enough for my neighbour, as she elbowed me again and gesture towards the front of the room.

"Go on!" she insisted.

"I'll think about it," I demurred. The last thing I wanted was to have any attention drawn to me, but she obviously didn't agree. My lovely neighbour is a wonderfully warm woman

Redemption

and always seems to have a bright smile on her face, but it would be a mistake to think she is a pushover in any way. She is one determined character with some very strong opinions and, I found out at that moment, she also has extremely pointy elbows. It was quite clear that she was going to ensure that I drew myself to the attention of Lady Awesome whether I liked it or not. It soon became evident that, if I wanted to avoid extreme bruising or a couple of broken ribs from those elbows I mentioned, I was going to have to give in graciously. In a desperate attempt to protect my torso and make sure she didn't announce her idea to the whole room, I whispered hastily, "I promise, I will speak to her afterwards, but let's allow her to finish up and have a cup of tea first, she must be exhausted."

"Hmm," she replied ominously before nodding meaningfully at me, in the same way that my mum does when she is really saying: "You'd better see that you do young lady because I'll be watching you!" Honestly, it was as if my mother was sat right there beside me in the hall in east Dorset, instead of two counties away causing mischief and mayhem for the residents of Devon.

Lady Awesome wound up her presentation to thunderous applause very shortly after that and there was a general increase in the noise level in the hall as the fifty or so ladies of the WI, who had been engrossed by the talk, were now gripped by a sudden need for caffeine. The usual refined scramble for the excellent home-baked refreshments ensued.

In the confusion that followed, I had every hope that I could avoid having to make good on my promise. I made a few fake moves in the general direction of Lady Awesome to try and throw my neighbour off the scent, feeling sure that she would eventually become engrossed in acquiring a cup of tea and a chocolate cupcake, but to no avail. She was wise to my little tricks and kept her eye on me at all times. At one point, from across the room, she even raised her eyebrows and pointed at her watch before crossing her arms and nodding forcefully in the direction she felt I should be moving. I couldn't help but quail inside. Obviously, I was not going to get away with my cunning plan of avoidance, but there was a whole group of very talented ladies of the WI lining up to chat to Lady Awesome already so I couldn't see why she would want to talk to me.

Eventually, as my lovely neighbour made a really obvious shooing gesture and moved as if to walk over there herself, I threw my hands up in the air in supplication and finally joined the back of the pack by the speaker.

All joking aside, what I didn't realise was that I was at one of those significant turning points in my life. You probably know the sort I mean, they are often unexpected and massively important when you look at things retrospectively, but at the time you generally don't recognise them for what they are. It's only with hindsight that you can see that they are fairly pivotal to future developments. With that reasoning, the next few minutes of my life were about to be quite momentous for me, if not in quite the way my lovely neighbour anticipated.

I edged closer to Lady Awesome, as the rest of the WI members eventually trotted off to dive on the refreshments, and told myself that my neighbour only had to think that I had told the speaker about my book. I didn't actually have to do it. Lady Awesome turned to me with a welcoming smile

Redemption

and said hello. I thanked her nervously for a great presentation and asked if I could buy a signed copy of the book that she was selling that evening before realising in mortification that I didn't have any money on me.

She laughed, signed a copy of her book with a flourish and handed it to me saying not to worry; I could transfer the money to her when I got home.

"You trust me?" I asked surprised.

"You look trustworthy enough to me," she said firmly and handed me her business card with her BACs details on the back. Taking it, I thanked her and watched as she started to pack her projector and laptop away as efficiently as she had on arrival.

I am not quite sure what came over me at that point, but seeing this compelling, inspirational woman gather her things together and make ready to leave, I was unexpectedly overcome by the urge to tell her my story. However, my window of opportunity to do so was disappearing before my eyes. I suddenly remembered the copy of my book that always lurked in the bottom of my handbag and, scrabbling around in the depths of the fabric, hurriedly drew it out. I held it out to Lady Awesome muttering, "Do you mind if I give you this? It's my story, based on true events." Then before she could really respond either way, I practically chucked the thing at her and said a quick goodbye before scarpering for the loos, where I then kicked myself hard (metaphorically) for being a socially inept idiot.

"Well! That went well," said my subconscious sarcastically. "You displayed a staggering lack of confidence there and covered yourself in glory...not! She's going to think you're a weirdo."

"Oh, do shut up," I begged. Fortunately, all the cubicles were empty so there was no danger of me scaring any more little old ladies by talking to myself this time. I was fully aware that I hadn't handled the situation with any kind of aplomb and I had no idea why. I only usually get tongue-tied like that over things that are really important. Maybe my book meant more to me than I realised.

Looking at myself in the mirror over the hand basin I wrinkled my nose, sighed and said, "Well, she'll either read it or she won't. It's not the end of the world if she doesn't."

"True, no harm done!" replied my subconscious quietly in a moment of unexpected solidarity. I shrugged and then pulled my handbag more securely onto my shoulder before going over to peer out of the ladies room door in order to see if the coast was clear so that I could make my escape to the car and go home.

Unknown to me, Lady Awesome was intrigued (in spite of my poor communication skills) and that was soon going to lead on to some very interesting developments indeed.

6. Inquisition

Definition: **A religious tribunal instigated by Pope Gregory IX in the twelfth century, notorious for prolonged and intense questioning and the use of torture to gain results**

Back to the Spanish Inquisition from the student in the past...

I wasn't going to get much of a reprieve from my offspring-induced interrogation. Logic isn't the type to let a subject go until she has finished with it to her full satisfaction; a quality that I completely admire when it isn't aimed at me. I couldn't hide in that grotty student accommodation kitchen forever. Unfortunately!

Let's not forget that when dropping a child off at university for the start of a new term it is also the dutiful parent's express obligation to feed the starving student. It's in the unwritten rulebook; the one that keeps changing to ensure that you are always in the wrong. The abandoning parent must provide a sufficiently large final meal in order to keep the student nourished throughout the weeks of hardship and study to come, before deserting them and beating a hasty retreat home at all speed. Hence, I found myself sat opposite Logic in the local pub an hour later watching her diligently work her way through a suitably sustaining, hearty student meal deal.

As she daintily chomped through a double beef burger loaded with extra bacon and cheese oozing out of an outsized bun, set in a vast sea of chips and deep fried onion rings complete with a single lettuce leaf one slice of cucumber and two segments of tomato on the side (no doubt this was supposed to be the healthy balanced bit of the whole meal), she came to the point with her usual tact, declaring emphatically, "Quiet is worried you'll get bored if you're not working."

Noting her strategic use of the 'blame-a-sibling' diversionary tactic, I couldn't help smiling wryly, because the subtext on that one was so obvious. What Quiet was really worried about was that I might start interfering in what he was up to with greater frequency and effect if I didn't have a job to keep me otherwise occupied. The last thing a sixteen-year old boy wants is a mother with too much time on her hands, hence there had been any number of suggestions from my older son with regard to possible jobs that he felt I should consider applying for. Funnily enough I wasn't enamoured with the idea of stacking shelves at the local supermarket full-time or working shifts at the local fast food joint except as a last resort. Nevertheless, Small thought the latter idea was fantastic until I explained that such a job would not mean he had access to an unlimited supply of free burgers.

"I don't think that's really what your brother is concerned about," I replied dryly.

She smiled. "It may not be his main motivation, I'll admit that, but I do think he is genuinely concerned about you. We all are."

"Really?" I asked in surprise, "There's no need, I'll find something. I'm just not sure what to go for at the moment."

"That is precisely the problem," she said emphatically.

Mystified, I replied, "I don't follow you."

Redemption

"It's your attitude, 'I'll find something,' for goodness' sake mum, you're forty-six not sixteen!"

Inhaling deeply, a bit taken aback by her exasperated tone, I said with studied patience, "Believe me, I am very aware of exactly how old I am."

"Shouldn't you know what you want to do with your life by now? You've been doing that office job for years and you've never particularly liked it. This is an opportunity for change. You need to do some serious thinking so that you make the right choice next. Start thinking about what you do want to do with the rest of your life." We (I mean she) had moved onto dessert by this time and she was stabbing viciously at a chocolate ice cream sundae using a teaspoon with a remarkably elongated handle, while I stared at her (and it) in bemusement. Just who exactly was the parent here? Shouldn't we be having this conversation the other way around?

I suddenly felt like I was sixteen again and not in a good way. (For me sixteen had involved a lot of puppy fat, pimples and a shocking poodle perm!) I had a nightmare flashback of the old teenage me sat opposite the remarkably uninspiring, elderly, fat and balding careers guidance counsellor; the one who told me categorically that going to art school was a really stupid idea, and to stop wasting my time because I would never make it as an artist. He then breezily recommended that I think about doing a typing course to become a secretary or perhaps consider nursing. The latter suggestion was a singularly bad idea given the number of times I had fainted that term in biology dissection classes.

Alice May

On reflection, I think that particular gentleman had spent years giving that same generic gender-biased careers advice to all the girls that had the misfortune to cross his path. He was probably correct in his assessment that I was unlikely to earn enough to live on through art. I really wasn't that good, hence my desire to go to college and learn how to be better. Nevertheless, his grumpy assertion that I should get my head out of the clouds like a good girl and get on with learning to type (with the subtext being that I could get an admin job until I got married and my husband could support me) had really annoyed me even then. Nowadays, such an archaic, anti-parity viewpoint is almost too painful to type but in the interests of honesty, there it is in black and white.

Defiantly chucking away the leaflet he gave me entitled 'Opportunities in Administration', and with my very supportive parents' encouragement, I applied to study environmental sciences at university instead because I was quite good at biology and geography. Nevertheless, his damning indictment that I would never make it as an artist had lodged itself very firmly in my brain.

Here I was, nearly thirty years later, discussing future employment suitability once again; only this time with a modern, more enlightened and, fortunately, more positive twist to it, because then Logic got down to the nitty-gritty and she doesn't beat about the bush.

"Seriously! I've lost count of the number of times you've said that you always wanted to be a full-time artist. This could be your opportunity. Why haven't you organised another exhibition? The last one was really quite successful, and I know the gallery want you back again. Chaos got an email from them. She sent it onto you and copied me in. You

Redemption

should follow it up. You'll have plenty of time soon to do that sort of thing."

"There's no money in art," I said unconsciously, reiterating exactly what the guidance counsellor had said all those years ago. Isn't it amazing how the things we absorbed when we were young stay with us? Subliminal social conditioning is responsible for inhibiting us in all sorts of ways, not all of them good, perpetuating unhealthy situations and attitudes down the generations without us even being aware of it.

"There won't be any money in it if you don't ever get your work out of your studio and in front of potential customers. Honestly Mum! How can anyone buy one of your paintings if they can't see them? You have to put them on display and give them a chance. Share them with the world. Why are you hiding them away? You tell us that we can do anything we want if we are prepared to work hard and go for it. We just want you to do the same."

"This is a bit different," I said.

"Why?" she asked, "I don't see how. Your paintings are beautiful. They tell a true and inspiring story that gives them an added meaning. What was it that lady at the exhibition said to you when she bought one of your fish paintings?" There was a pause while Logic went a bit cross-eyed as she tried to remember. I looked at her with interest, wondering absently if she could actually see through both eyes at the same time when she did that.

"That was it!" I jumped, startled, as her eyes suddenly snapped back to their usual straight alignment and skewered me in my seat as she continued. "She said she'd had a really tough time recently and that your fish painting made her feel that there was light at the end of the tunnel and that it represented hope to her."

I nodded slowly not really sure where this conversation was going, "Yes, she did seem to quite like it."

"But then you went and tried to give her the painting for nothing!"

"Well, I wanted her to have it, if it meant that much to her."

"Luckily for you she wouldn't accept it as a gift and went off to pay for it properly through the gallery."

I shrugged, muttering "I don't see why I couldn't just give it to her."

Logic sighed heavily yet again, "Because if you did that, you would devalue it, for yourself and for her. You have to appreciate what your paintings are worth and price them accordingly. If you don't value yourself, no-one else is going to. You have a real skill and create genuinely original work, paintings that speak to people. Painting is not some little hobby to you is it?"

I thought about that for a while, considering the obsessively overwhelming need that I experienced to complete each piece, before saying quietly, yet definitely, "No, my painting is not a hobby. It's never been a hobby."

"Start valuing yourself then and get your work out there. We all believe in you, but if you don't believe in yourself then it doesn't count for anything does it? Chaos is ready and

Redemption

waiting to negotiate a second exhibition with the gallery for you, and to approach others. You just need to say the word, OK?"

There was a long silence while she tipped the sundae glass up to her lips and drained the dregs of cream, chocolate and melted ice cream. Returning the empty glass to the table she grinned and said, "Just think about it, please, for us? But more importantly for you OK? That's all I'm asking."

***

And that is exactly what I did! I thought about future opportunities all the way home, as I pootled across Devon and Dorset on the A35 behind a succession of slow-moving vehicles, including lumbering lorries, trundling tractors and countless crawling caravans. I thought about what Logic had said and realised that she had a fair point when she said that my self-esteem was on the low side. I didn't know why that was but suspected that it had a lot to do with having had the stuffing mentally knocked out of me when the house had fallen down. It was definitely affecting my decisions and not necessarily in a good way. I was going to have to find a way to work on that.

Furthermore, why on earth was I still allowing the echoing words of a myopic, misogynistic careers counsellor from thirty years ago to affect me? If I were advising any of my children in my situation, I would tell them to believe in themselves and go for it. Could it actually be time for me to take a risk? Should I step out from the shadows of the past and start making the long-buried dreams of my sixteen-year-old self, to become a full -time artist, a reality? I came to the conclusion that, yet again, my Barbarian advisory team were on to something. This was an opportunity that I would be a fool to miss. I wasn't quite sure exactly what I was going to do yet or how I was going to do it, but it was definitely time to consider a new approach.

As Daisy and I pootled around the Dorchester ring road I had moved on in my mental musings to contemplate the story behind the paintings and the emotional journey I had been on as I created them. There was clear imagery of healing behind the sequence of canvases, each having been created as I climbed painfully slowly out of the dangerously deep pit of despair I had plummeted into after the house and our lives had collapsed around us. My paintings had helped that broken version of me to heal and, when seen together as a complete collection, they represented a visual voyage of my struggle up from the darkness of shock and depression into a light, bright future of hope, all created with oil paint, acrylic, watercolour and canvas.

My paintings told a powerful tale. They told the saga of the house that sat down. But it was the concept of actually telling that story that stayed in the forefront of my mind for the remainder of the journey home.

7. Modification

Definition: the process of making of minor or gradual, small changes to something

*Returning to the **present** day, shortly after meeting Lady Awesome at the WI….*

The morning that followed the incredible presentation at the Women's Institute, having spent a large part of the night annoying Beloved Husband by keeping the light on so I could read Lady Awesome's book, I woke far earlier than normal. The book turned out to be an entertaining yet knowledgeable guide to finding self-confidence and unlocking your true potential as a working woman, and considering I had low self-esteem issues, it was quite a timely read for me. Now normally I don't particularly go for self-help-guide-type books, but this was not like that at all. It was actually a very amusing read, with chapters on setting achievable goals and strategies for success, whilst still coping with life and associated family-related complications. It was rather a shame I hadn't read it before I'd had the kids, or at least whilst I still had a job to go to. That last thought trotted through my mind as I sat at the breakfast bar, yawning rather rudely at my Marmite on toast.

It was with some surprise, given the fact that it was 6.30am, that I saw the door onto the patio suddenly open and Quiet entered the house from the garden. I did my best to hide the confusion I felt at the fact that not only had he been outside, but he had obviously been up and dressed for quite some time, a previously unheard of phenomenon. Instead of making a big deal about it, I casually offered him a cup of tea.

"No thanks, I've just had one," he replied with a quick smile as he placed an empty cup in the sink. Now I was really intrigued about what on earth had taken him outside so early for long enough to drink an entire cup of tea. Strange behaviour indeed!

"Really? Where have you been?" I couldn't help myself. I had to ask.

"Oh, just outside," he answered and looked at me with genuine astonishment, as if that should have been obvious.

Before I could start a subtle campaign of maternal interrogation (OK, probably not so subtle), he spiked my guns by leaving the room and I could hear him bounding up the stairs, several treads at a time, and then his door closed very firmly. It would seem that my curiosity was going to have to wait for the moment. I made a mental note to revisit this information later before turning my attention back to my original morning musings and my, now cold and rubbery, toast with a small dissatisfied exclamation.

"Humph!"

It was now my third week of being officially unemployed and I still had no idea what I was actually going to do to earn money. I had given a great deal of thought to the advice Logic had given me about expanding the exhibition side of my art and, while it was great fun selling paintings and a great motivator for creating more, it wasn't proving a sufficiently reliable way to earn a living. I had put together another exhibition over the Christmas period having followed up the invitation I had received from the gallery

Redemption

after the first event, and there was another one in the pipeline for the summer months. However, as a source of income it was erratic. I needed a way to generate more opportunities to put my work before a wider audience more regularly, but I didn't quite know how to go about that. While I had a gut reaction that there was a way to make this work, it felt like I was missing something obvious. It was as if something was lurking at the corner of my eye where I couldn't quite see it and, even if I turned my head, I couldn't bring it into my field of vision; yet it was definitely there.

It was also quite annoying that I wasn't able to take advantage of my 'lack of a job' situation by having a nice long lie-in in the mornings. For the first time in I don't know how long, I didn't have to be in the office by 9am, but the boy Barbarians still had to get to school and Beloved Husband left too early in the morning to take them in. Now that Quiet was sixteen and in the sixth form doing A-levels, he no longer qualified for a free place on the school bus but wasn't old enough to learn to drive himself there. Not that we could afford a car for him anyway. The upshot of this was that even though I didn't have to get up to go to work in the mornings, I still had to get up to do the school run because it was way cheaper than buying Quiet a bus pass.

Small would often cadge a lift in with me too, even though, being under the age of sixteen, he did qualify for a free bus pass. (I know! The rules make no sense whatsoever, which is no great surprise when you think about it. Two boys, both in full-time education, living at the same address, going to the same school couldn't possibly *both* get a bus pass could they? That would be daft!) It had only taken Small a second to work out that travelling to school in Daisy every morning was a much more comfortable option to walking more than two miles to stand on his own, at a bus stop on the edge of a random field, in the middle of nowhere on a cold, dark, often rainy, early January morning. He's not daft.

Anyway, I was still pondering what to do about potentially boosting my income stream after I had dropped both boys to school and returned to the empty house. As I blew the steam of a restorative cup of lemon and green tea, I couldn't help remembering some of the more entertaining aspects of Lady Awesome's presentation from the evening before. She'd seemed so confident and comfortable that she made the whole public speaking thing look easy. I was convinced that because she was relaxed and appeared to be enjoying herself, it had encouraged the audience to relax and enjoy themselves too and I wished I knew how to do something similar. I'd had another phone call from my mother recently and there was no way she was going to let me off the hook with this Literary and Creative Society talk she had signed me up for, so I was just jolly well going to have to get on with it.

In that weird way that can often happen, it was as if by thinking about Lady Awesome I had conjured her up, because my phone pinged to alert me to a new email and in seconds there on the screen in my hand was a message from her. I had emailed her as soon as I'd got home from the WI and completed that promised BACs payment for her, just to confirm that the payment had gone through. Her response this morning was warm and friendly, thanking me for the payment and telling me that she'd been up late the night before reading my book.

Redemption

A good feeling spread through me, perhaps she didn't think I was a nutter after all. It was nice that we'd both been up reading each other's books at the same time.

She finished her email by asking if I would be interested in going along to a small informal meeting of the Brilliant Women in Business Brunch Group in two days' time, suggesting that this would be a low-key gathering I might enjoy where I could get to know some other local women who would be attending.

Before I could even begin to think of all the reasons why I couldn't go, my obstinate inner identity piped up, "Don't you dare find an excuse! You need to expand your customer base remember? You might make some really useful contacts at a meeting like this. If you can survive the house falling down and all the nonsense that went on afterwards, then a bit of brunch with some businesswomen should be a doddle! Grow a backbone girl!"

With visions of my mother, my lovely neighbour and my own subconscious ganging up on me if I even considered not going, I straightened my spine, pulled my shoulders back and gave in to the inevitable. If I am totally frank, I think I was even secretly looking forward to it; I was getting rather bored on my own at home all day. I could do this!

With some surprise that I had successfully managed to kick myself up my own backside, I sent a polite acceptance back to Lady Awesome and booked the meeting into my empty, newly-unemployed person's diary.

8. Inducement
Definition: **The thing that leads someone into action or encourages momentum forward.**

*Continuing in the **present** and the meeting of the Brilliant Women in Business ....*

Hmmm! So much for my new-found backbone! It hadn't lasted long. All I'd had to do was rock up at the venue for the breakfast meeting ten minutes early. Actually, if I am completely honest it was twenty minutes, but I get stressed if I'm late and I was worried I might not be able to park, so the result was that I was far too early. Sadly, this meant I had too much time to lurk uncertainly outside the door of the conference room that the receptionist had directed me to and worry about what might be waiting for me on the other side. That was when the metaphorical mind monkeys hopped onto my shoulder and started whispering their poison into my ear to undermine my confidence. What was I doing here? I wasn't a businesswoman. I was unemployed for goodness sake. I would be totally out of place and wouldn't know what to say. I'd better leave now before I embarrassed myself.

What a time for my stroppy subconscious to take a sudden sabbatical! I needed her to back me up here, to tell the mind-monkeys to naff off and leave me alone. Then perhaps she could give me a bit of a stern talking to while she was at it, I thought hopefully and waited for some input from her. Sadly, she remained stubbornly silent.

I ummed and ahhed for a good few minutes while shifting from foot to foot nervously. Just as I was concluding that I

Redemption

probably should just give up and go home, I registered the tantalising aroma of warm croissants permeating the air and my stomach rumbled insistently. There had been no time this morning to indulge in any more than half a cup of tea, gulped down in passing before I had shuffled my reluctant Barbarians off to school (way earlier than usual) so that I could continue on to track down the location for this meeting. I was to wonder later if my hunger had contributed to my pathetic indecisiveness about entering the room, but the comforting scent of freshly-baked croissants was to prove just the inducement I needed, and something quite extraordinary happened. Involuntarily my back straightened and I drew myself up nice and tall. Smoothing down my hair quickly and taking a deep breath, my right hand reached for the door and pushed firmly. Two seconds later I was through the doorway and standing in a puddle of warm, bright sunshine that poured down from a series of huge windows marching along the length of an enormous room.

Blinking as my eyes adjusted to the sudden brilliance, I had no time to wonder what on earth I was going to do or say, because Lady Awesome herself welcomed me the instant I appeared and enveloped me in a quick warm hug.

"You made it! You're nice and early too, so you can pick the best seat. Come on in and grab yourself a coffee."

She gestured over to a long table covered in a crisp, white cloth on which was set out a mountain of breakfast goodies, including a large tray of the aforementioned croissants. "Let me just sign you in, give you a badge and then I'll introduce you."

Alice May

I had no idea to whom she planned to introduce me, because my first dazzled impression was that there wasn't anyone else there. However, my eyes slowly started to function properly again whilst I poured myself a cup of coffee and, when I turned around to survey the rest of the room, I could see one other person present, a woman with the most incredible pink hair. Not a puny, pathetic pastel pink either, I am talking about serious, mind-blowingly magnificent, 'don't mess with me' magenta! That statement colour echoed through her funky outfit too and emanated through her aura. I don't really understand the whole 'aura' thing, it's not usually something that features on my radar, but this woman definitely had one and it was undeniably pink. Just looking at her made my fingers start to twitch in artistic anguish at the lack of paints and brushes in my immediate environment. Here was a woman who exuded confidence, character, charisma and caring all by simply existing, and I instinctively wanted to capture that energetic essence on canvas.

Lady Awesome escorted me across the thick burgundy carpet towards the large conference table and made a quick introduction before excusing herself because there were more women starting to spill through the door behind us.

"Hello," said Magenta (what else could she be called?) with a bright smile. "Are you joining me?" I nodded nervously before setting my bag on the back of the chair next to hers and sitting down. "So, what do you do?" she asked.

"Oh!" I stammered. "Not that much really, I'm kind of between jobs, not sure what my next step is. I paint. I don't actually have a business, so I probably shouldn't really be here, sorry."

Redemption

"You're exploring some options are you? Don't apologise for that, we've all been there at some time or another. What would you like to do if you could?"

"Oh well, I'd like to be an artist. Properly. Full-time. I do sell quite a bit of work, but it's a fairly erratic income, dependant on exposure, exhibitions that sort of thing. I've been relying on an office job for a regular wage until recently. But that's over now."

"But surely if you paint and sell original work then you are already an artist."

"I don't have any art qualifications."

"Who cares? The real question is 'can you paint?' If you can and it's what you want to do, then you should do it. Life is too short to do a job you hate unless you have no other choice. Lots of the women who come to these groups are running their own kitchen table companies. Businesses that are based on things they feel passionately about. They're often working at other jobs at the same time to help pay the bills too."

"Really?"

"Yes, sometimes it's the only way to get what you really want to do off the ground at the start."

That was interesting, so I wasn't the only one spinning several plates whilst dreaming of a simpler but more satisfying future.

Alice May

Just at that moment, Lady Awesome whizzed over to our table to collect some papers and as she did so she grinned at us asking, "How are you ladies getting on?" She looked at Magenta but jerked her head at me before continuing, "Has she told you about the book she wrote yet?"

"You wrote a book?" Magenta rounded on me, her eyes fairly popping out of her head in outraged delight.

"I was up all night reading it," confirmed Lady Awesome. "Couldn't put it down! Oh look, another arrival, excuse me, I'll be back in a minute." She whisked back off across the room to coax another lady, also tentatively poking her nose through the door, to come in and raid the coffee supplies. The sight of someone else who was clearly a bit unsure of herself made me feel less out of place.

"So, you're an artist and an author," said Magenta archly.

"I'm not really an author," I demurred. "I just wrote a book. It was only a bit of fun."

"What do you mean you 'just' wrote a book?" she demanded with a quizzical expression on her face.

"Well…. I ….." I wasn't really sure what to say. "I don't think many people have actually bought it."

"No-one's going to want to buy it if you run it down like that. It's a massive achievement to write a book. I couldn't write one. Most people haven't written one. You need to say it like this," she paused, dramatically, squared her shoulders, took a deep breath and continued speaking as she threw her arms out in a melodramatic but commanding gesture and spoke.

"I wrote a book!"

Her tone was positive, firm yet warm and her statement was clear, concise and had a significant lift in pitch at the end. She smiled warmly at me and then said in her normal voice, "I'm a voice coach. Can you tell?"

"I'd never have guessed!" I teased.

"So, you're an author and an artist. You should be proud of that. That's cool! What sort of thing do you paint?"

"Well, anything that takes my fancy really. Oils, acrylics, watercolours, it depends on the effect I want. I painted the images for the cover of the book too, which was fun." I paused suddenly as a penny dropped at the back of my mind. I'd suddenly caught a slightly clearer glimpse of that thing that had been nagging at the corner of my eye. Shaking my head, I dragged my mind back to the conversation at hand so as not to appear rude but made a quick mental note to pursue that 'dropped penny' at a later date.

"Now we're getting somewhere! You wrote a book and you painted the artwork for it yourself, and yet you tell me you're not a real artist or a real author. For goodness' sake woman! Own your achievements! Don't run them down. There are plenty of people out there who will do the negative stuff for you." She shook her head at me wryly before continuing, "We've really got our work cut out with you, haven't we?"

Alice May

"What do you mean?"

"Confidence my girl, that's what you need. A good dose of self-confidence! But don't you worry. We'll soon sort you out. Have you brought a copy of your book then?" my vibrant new friend demanded.

"Oh! Yes, sorry," I dug around in my bag for one, feeling just a little bit steamrolled but, surprisingly, I didn't feel like running for the hills, which would be my usual response under such circumstances.

"Oh dear, you're one of those as well." She shook her head sadly, but I could see a twinkle in her eye.

"One of what?" I had to ask. It would have been rude not to and anyway I was rather intrigued as to what this entertainingly nutty character would say next. She didn't seem to have any traditional conversation boundaries. Although going by her extraordinarily vivid hair, why on earth would I expect her to be conventional?

"You're an 'apologiser', you keep saying 'sorry' when you don't need to. Don't apologise for your book. It's not some kind of mistake. You didn't write it by accident. If you don't value it then you can't expect anyone else to. You're not really sorry, so don't say it."

"Are you going to tell me off all day?" I asked looking into my empty coffee cup as it dawned on me that I might be requiring considerably more caffeine to cope with the rest of this morning.

Redemption

"Probably," she agreed with an irrepressible smile. "It's what I do. You'll just have to put up with it. Or move seats of course. I won't be offended."

I decided I quite liked her refreshingly blunt approach. I'd love to have even an ounce of her poise and assurance, and she did have a point. It was very easy to get into the habit of saying sorry. To constantly excuse yourself and your accomplishments.

"Well, I think I'll be just fine right here." I said.

"Jolly good! Oh look, I think we are about to start."

The room had filled up with a fair selection of smart looking women all chattering away to each other while Magenta and I had been indulging in that bit of barmy banter and Lady Awesome had greeted them all. She was now approaching the head of the conference table in order to begin proceedings. The meeting started in earnest with each of the ladies standing up in turn and introducing themselves and their businesses with a quick one minute spiel. Listening to them, I marvelled that I was there at all, it was a totally new and unanticipated environment but it wasn't an unwelcome one. In actual fact it was quite inspiring. I was definitely panicking about what on earth I was going to say when it came to my turn to stand up, but the positivity in the room was incredible.

All too quickly it was my turn and I started shaking even before I got to my feet. Mumbling my name and a few random sentences about looking for new opportunities, I sat down as quickly as I could and Magenta nudged me and leaned over to whisper, "Well done, that was a good first try.

Alice May

It's called an 'Elevator Pitch'. There's a real art to doing it effectively. Make sure you come to the next meeting, I'll be running a workshop on how to put them together to make the most effective use of the time."

I knew she was being kind. There was no way my pathetic attempt to emulate the women around me had been any good at all, but I didn't feel embarrassed like I would normally. No-one was laughing at me; many ladies were actively nodding and smiling. In fact, the whole group seemed genuinely intent on encouraging and supporting each other. I could feel my horizons opening up before me with potential opportunities as I sat there listening to them all. It was the most surreal feeling.

Later on, with only half an ear on the closing minutes of the meeting, I examined that 'falling penny' in the back of my mind a little closer. It kept nagging away at me, and in light of the bizarre conversation with Magenta and the inspiration of the women around me, I realised that I needed to look at my skill set in a more holistic way, rather than compartmentalising things. In fact, there might be a way for them to complement each other. The book and the art were both very creative and told the same basic story using different media. Perhaps they could work together somehow, each strengthening the other. At the grand old age of forty-six, it seemed that I was at last putting the pieces of my personal puzzle together and was ready to find out what I was going to be when I finally grew up.

Looking at the copy of my book on the table before me, I recalled the day that the writing had started so unexpectedly. As little as five minutes before I began to type, I hadn't realised what I was going to do. Even as I was

Redemption

tapping away at the keyboard, a part of my brain was asking quite stridently what on earth I thought I was doing. This was not normal for me, I didn't write, I painted but still I had kept on going. It was completely out of character, but once I started I found it felt so right that I couldn't stop, so I kept going. Even as I was writing I kept expecting to run out of things to say and thought that my typing would eventually grind to an ignominious halt, but it didn't.

This uncharacteristic phenomenon had all started shortly after I had cleared out my studio room, on Patience's recommendation, in order to make it more viewing friendly. It was only a day or so after my trip back from Devon, following Logic's interrogation of me about my future plans and her comments about my paintings telling a story. I don't think that she had any concept that the little pep talk she had delivered to me over lunch in the pub would trigger such a reaction (neither had I for that matter), but that was exactly what happened.

9. Adaptation

Definition: a specific process of change to meet altered circumstances

*Returning to the **past**, approximately thirty-six hours after my return from Devon...*

"What on earth is she doing?" The not very hushed whisper hissed from the doorway behind me.

There was a pause and then a shuffling sound.

"Uuuum!" Came a second, deeper, hushed voice, "Well.... it looks like she's typing!"

"What, you mean like on a computer?"

More shuffling.

"Yup!"

"Why?"

"Well how should I know?" The deeper voice came out more impatiently this time.

"I didn't know she could do that." The first voice expressed a degree of muted outrage!

Part of my mind was registering the hushed conversation taking place behind me and found it quite amusing that Small was surprised that I might have skills of which he was previously unaware. Admittedly I wasn't obviously the most

Redemption

technologically minded of parents but what on earth did he think I did all day at work? Use chalk and a slate to send messages? I might not know much about social media or be able to send text messages from my phone using both thumbs at the speed of light like teenagers could, but my typing skills were something I was quite proud of.

Honed back in the late 80's thanks to a combination of the advent of 'Mavis Beacon' and a need to get university summer vacation work to reduce my overdraft, my ability to touch type is something that has proven extremely useful over the years. Nevertheless, I normally kept this skill under wraps because I had learned the hard way that if your colleagues know you can touch type, you generally get all the typing jobs dumped on your desk and subsequently end up missing out on more exciting projects. Always, always make them do their own typing, it's good for them.

Anyway, back to the unsubtle discussion going on behind me. I was so focused on my 'scandalous' typing, that I was only vaguely listening to them.

"What should we do?" asked Small

There was another pause before Quiet answered him.
"I think we should make a sandwich."

"Good idea!" There was a pause before Small continued, sounding a bit concerned, "But we don't know what she wants in it!"

"Not for her, you dummy! For us! I'm starving!"

"Oh! OK! That's a really good idea!" Small agreed before adding, "Hey! Don't call me dummy!"

The noise of scuffling ensued as the boys abandoned me for the delights of raiding the fridge. I could hear them shoving each other playfully into furniture as they raced to reach the kitchen first. Having recently restocked, I knew there was plenty in the fridge and, as such, there was no danger of them starving, so I tuned them out and focused fully on what I was doing.

My Barbarian boys' observational skills were absolutely spot on! I was typing. Now normally, as you know, I'd be painting but I was not painting today, hence the boys' astonishment. When I had got home from my shift at work having done the school pick-up en route, I had felt totally dispirited. It had been really hard to focus in the office earlier with the knowledge that I was surplus to requirements for the company's future, hence an intense feeling of disengagement had settled heavily on my shoulders and it was hard to shake off even now. I stood in my unnaturally tidy art studio and looked around.

It had been nearly ten days since the big studio de-clutter. Ten days in which I had barely been able to bring myself to enter the room. It was too organised. I daren't get anything out. If I started to work on a new piece I knew the whole room would be trashed in no time, so my instinctive impulse to create was crushed by my knowledge that the need to find a buyer was far more important and, therefore, for the first time in ages I felt no craving to paint which worried me because even though there was no spark to paint crackling in my fingers, my head felt absolutely full to the point of bursting. Confusingly though, it was not full of the usual

Redemption

things like images, shapes and colours anymore; this time my head felt as if it was full of something else entirely, something that had never particularly interested me before.

Words.

Lots of words.

Words and phrases had been building up in my mind over the last few days, since my return from Devon. Clauses kept creeping up on me when I should have been thinking about other things (like my soon-to-be-gone job). Grammatical constructions were starting to spill over themselves in my brain in waves, constantly multiplying, then lurking and waiting to pounce on me at unsuspecting moments, until my skull felt like it was on the point of exploding with expressions that wanted to escape.

I didn't understand it, but there was only one thing I could think of to do with them all. The scenarios that were playing themselves out, over and over again, on a loop inside my mind had to be excised somehow. If I couldn't paint, then I was going to have to find another way to create. As is often the way with me, I acted on basic instinct and simply followed the impulse. I decided that I was going to have to write the words down in the hope that they would then leave me in peace.

Turning my back on my art materials, I dug around in the bottom drawer of the filing cabinet and eventually emerged with an old laptop that Logic had left behind when she first went away to university the year before. I placed it on the desk by the window and plugged it in before pressing the 'on' button. It wasn't long before I had booted up Word and that was when I started to type.

Weirdly enough, I wasn't really conscious of what I was typing particularly, I was merely aware that the pressure in my head was easing and so my fingers kept hitting the keys, settling into a steady, rhythmic pace. The onslaught of words continued as they organised themselves neatly into sentences. Those sentences became paragraphs and then paragraphs became pages. You get the general idea, I'm sure.

Time passed. Quite a lot of time actually, which is why my boys had come looking for me, ostensibly to find out why I hadn't cooked them any supper, resulting in the conversation from the doorway behind me with regard to what I was doing. Grateful that they had decided to feed themselves (something I knew they were more than capable of doing), I focused on typing for a bit longer.

I kept meaning to stop, but never did.

Eventually the noise of the front door opening to admit Beloved Husband before being firmly shut and locked filtered into my conscious mind. This was followed by the sound of him stomping along the hall into the kitchen whilst jettisoning coat, shoes and briefcase along the way. The audible reverberation of the fridge opening and then closing followed by a few cupboard doors doing the same reached me. He was probably searching for the supper I hadn't made. Ooops!

Redemption

Heavy footsteps ambled past to the lounge and I heard him address the boys cheerfully, "You alright boys? Where's your mother?"

There was a pause as Quiet, no doubt, had to extricate his brain from whichever PlayStation game they were playing in order to answer his father, "Hi Dad! She's in the studio."

"Yeah," agreed Small. "She's typing." That particular phrase was uttered in a hushed, horror-filled whisper, as if I was indulging in something decidedly indecent.

"Oh, OK!" he said, and his footsteps sounded in the corridor again before stopping abruptly. "Hang on a minute! She's what?"

"She's typing," repeated Small.

"Really?" Beloved Husband sounded intrigued and I heard several pairs of footsteps, both little and large, approach the doorway of the studio and stop as all three of my menfolk studied me intently from the threshold.

"So she is!" Beloved Husband concluded with mild surprise. "Have you boys eaten?" he continued.

"We're starving!" chorused both boys together. What little fibbers! They couldn't possibly be starving! I had heard them make several raids on the kitchen in the time I had been working. It would be a minor miracle if there was any food left but, as is inevitable with teenage boys, well one teenager and one very-nearly-a-teenager, they both had two hollow legs each and were still hungry.

"OK!" Beloved Husband said, "I'll rustle up some beans on toast while we leave your mother get on with it."

"Get on with what though?" Quiet asked.

"I have absolutely no idea," he replied, not sounding remotely bothered. "But let's leave her alone to get on with it in peace, shall we? There's a football match starting on telly soon. If she's typing she won't badger us to change channel for something soppy." (For the record, I do not watch 'soppy' TV programmes; I simply occasionally prefer to see if there is something else on other than sport or gratuitous violence.)

Given the enthusiastic response that greeted the sports scheduling information, I realised that all curiosity with regard to my activities had been successfully diverted. Which was just as well because I didn't have clue why I was doing what I was doing, so how could I explain it? I just knew that I needed to do it and so the words kept coming.

Some not insignificant time later I felt a hand on my shoulder. Pausing for a second, I looked up from the screen, vaguely interested to note that it was now dark outside. Beloved Husband was standing next to me with a distinctly puzzled look on his face.

"Don't you think you should move around a bit? It can't be healthy to sit still for so long and don't say you are moving your fingers, it doesn't count. I've made you some food. Why don't you save that up and come through?" He patted my shoulder gently and left the room. "And whatever that is you are working on, have you been backing it up?" he called back casually.

Redemption

Daft man! Of course I hadn't! Who does he think I am? It was a good idea though. In a daze, I registered that it was nearly eleven o'clock at night. I had been typing for well over six hours. The document before me on the screen registered nearly 16,000 words. Feeling quite sure I had never written so much in such a short time ever before, I surreptitiously tested the inside of my head and realised that it was feeling better. Less congested. Which was good, but my eyes were sore from staring at the screen and I desperately needed a wee.

He was right, it was probably well past time to save what I had written and take a break. Scrabbling around in the desk drawer I found a memory stick and proceeded to save copies of the document onto both the desktop and the USB before closing the laptop down and heading for the kitchen to find a steaming bowl of tomato soup with a chunk of fresh bread and some cheese waiting for me.

Why is it that food you haven't had to prepare yourself tastes so heavenly? I chomped ravenously on the simple fare and then fell into bed in an exhausted but happy haze, sleeping dreamlessly for several hours, until the words started to nudge playfully at my sub-conscious again and the cycle of writing began again.

10. Transmutation
Definition: conversion from one form into another

*Let us continue with our heroine's bizarre typing activities in the **past**....*

"What time did you get up? It must have been incredibly early," muttered Beloved Husband in disgust, as he leaned past me to reach for a coaster so he could place a steaming mug of tea on the desk next to the laptop.

"Hmmm....! It wasn't that early, I just wanted to make a few notes before I do the school run." I was fudging it a little because, in reality, I'd been up for hours as I had woken at about two in the morning, itching to resume my typing. It was as if there was a film playing in my head, repeatedly, and it had persisted in pestering me, preventing me from dropping back off to sleep again. I thought that if I wrote down what was happening, then it might leave me alone long enough to get some sleep. So, I'd crept downstairs to the studio in the dead of night and switched the laptop back on. I'd been typing ever since. Just as I thought I was getting to the end of what I wanted to say, there were suddenly more words backing up in my mind, urging me on and making it impossible to turn the computer off.

Fortunately, I'd had the foresight to put on not only my own dressing gown, but also Beloved Husband's big black one, because it was extremely cold sat at the computer in the dark hours before dawn, in spite of the fact that it was only September. This unique sartorial selection was one of the reasons I then resembled an overweight grizzly bear ready to hibernate for winter. I never look terribly glamorous first

Redemption

thing in the morning (or ever, if I'm completely candid) but the combination of dark circles under my eyes courtesy of virtually no sleep, plus two thick fluffy dressing gowns, significantly increasing my girth, was never going to improve matters.

"What time is it?" I suddenly asked in alarm. If Beloved Husband was up and dressed then surely the boys should be too. If I wasn't careful I was going to be late getting them to school.

"Don't worry. I gave both boys a nudge about twenty minutes ago. Quiet's having breakfast and Small is packing his games kit. I'll take them in for you this morning. I've got a meeting first thing that'll take me past the school at the right sort of time anyway."

"Thanks," I breathed a sigh of relief and turned back to my screen. A hand on my shoulder stopped me.

"Just a suggestion though," he continued. "Perhaps you should take a shower and get dressed before you start that again. Why don't you set an alarm? I know it's your day off today, but don't forget there's a viewing at one o'clock this afternoon." He smiled and shrugged as if it didn't bother him either way before sauntering from the room.

***

Luckily, I'd followed his excellent advice, because it only felt like half an hour later that the alarm in the kitchen went off, alerting me to the fact that I had only a short time until Patience and the latest potential house buyer descended on the property for the viewing. It was time for a quick scoot round to check that the house was in a suitably neat condition. I had my suspicions that sufficient tidiness was unlikely, therefore I reluctantly turned off the computer and headed upstairs to check the bedrooms.

A few minutes later I peered into Small's room with rising dismay. He had obviously made a half-hearted attempted to straighten the room for the viewing before he went to school that morning, but his opinion on what made a tidy room differed wildly from mine.

Admittedly, there was nothing on the floor, but a suspiciously large bulge under the duvet gave away exactly where everything that usually resided on the floor was now concealed. Flipping the duvet to one side, I pulled a random collection of jumpers, trainers, pyjamas, Lego models, books, a mini wrench and a wind-up torch back on to the floor before re-making the bed properly. Then I shoved the pile of detritus over to the wardrobe with my foot and pulled open the cupboard door with every intention of scooping all the hanging clothes to one side and dumping in the haphazard jumble of Small's possessions, where they would be out of sight and able to be dealt with at some later date.

However, it was immediately apparent why Small hadn't used this space for all his junk, as there in the wardrobe was Skelly, dressed in a red and white stripy t-shirt and blue jeans. The Barbarians had evidently been playing a melded version of 'Hide and Seek' and 'Where's Wally?' with him. I sighed heavily. I'd forgotten about the 'scary Skelly' issue. Hauling him out of the wardrobe, I stuffed Small's collection of dubious treasures into the space and closed the door. Then I had to think fast. What was I going to do about Skelly?

Redemption

There was no way we were getting rid of him; he was part of the family. However, a temporary storage solution was definitely required. One that meant whoever was moving him around wouldn't know where he was and couldn't retrieve him until after we had a buyer. I needed Skelly to disappear for a bit. Not permanently, but it was time for him to have a little holiday. The question was where.

A short while later, I was dragging him, wrapped in an old blanket tied up with string, out of the front door towards the boot of my car. I had decided to lock him in there out of sight for the time being, where the boys couldn't find him until after we'd sold the house. Unfortunately, there were two flaws in my cunning plan. The first one was that I wasn't actually strong enough to get him into the car. Skeletons, whether fake or real, are an awkward shape and much heavier than they look! I did manage to lift his head and shoulders up and over the lip of the car boot, but when I reached down to try do the same with his feet, his upper body fell out again and I couldn't help but wince as his head hit the pea shingle with a bone-jarring crunch. That was when I realised my second problem - he wasn't going to fit in the boot space anyway because he wouldn't bend in the middle. I didn't want to use any force in case I hurt him. (Yes, I know he's not real, but that's not the point!)

Pausing in my exertions in order to re-think my strategy, I stood up to wipe the sweat from my forehead and froze in alarm! Standing stock still in the road at the entrance to our driveway were an elderly couple staring at me, transfixed with shock, as their beautiful brown and white beagle bounded over to sniff at the large, 'dead human' shaped bundle at my feet.

Appreciating, far too late, just how suspicious my actions must appear, I tried to brazen it out by smiling and nodding politely at them. "Lovely day for it, isn't it?" I asked, inwardly cringing.

What a stupid thing to say!

Lovely day for what exactly? A nice bit of murder? The hiding of corpses in the boot of the car perhaps?

Seriously?

Nevertheless, my comment seemed to break their horrified trance as the man nodded back very warily, then pulled at his companion's arm whilst calling dog to heel, before they scurried off in the direction of the village.

'Great!' I muttered to myself, 'that'll be all round the county by lunchtime and the fact that no-one wants to buy the house will be the least of my problems. If I'm not careful, the police will be round here with handcuffs and a team of forensic experts wanting to dig up the patio!'

Giving a heavy sigh, I closed the car boot and started to drag Skelly by the ankles across the drive towards the garage where I rolled him up in an old bit of carpet. (I know it's a cliché but carpeting really does disguise the distinct 'dead-body' shape of a ...well... a dead body so much better than a blanket does.) The carpet was a remnant left over from when the house had collapsed and had been abandoned there for no apparent reason, so I figured no-one would interfere with it anytime soon. Once Skelly was completely enshrouded, I stuffed him gently behind the massive pile of

Redemption

cricket equipment the boys had accumulated over the summer months. Dusting off my hands I headed back inside to have a last-minute scurry round the house looking for potential unmentionables before settling back at my laptop to wait for Patience to arrive with the latest viewers.

The immediate Scary Skelly issue was sorted! Or so I thought...

Part 3

'From a small seed a mighty trunk might grow'

Aeschylus 525BC – 456BC

11. Conversion
Definition: **an adaptation of something from one form to another, a process of change.**

*Let's return to the **present** for a bit and our heroine's attempts to gain more self-confidence.....*

By the time my first meeting with the Brilliant Women in Business group was over, I had rather a lot of things to think about.

Not only had I met some amazing people, all trying to do something they felt passionately about, I had also been on a crash course in assertiveness. The group was not merely for networking, making business contacts and chatting; there was also an educational element to the meeting, which had been about politely and firmly standing your ground if you needed to. Assertiveness was something that I now appreciated was significantly lacking in my general day-to-day demeanour. (This was a realisation that surprised me, because I used to be a fairly determined character when I was younger. My stroppy inner voice could well be a remnant of that former fortitude.)

This week was turning into a bit of a self-improvement binge-fest, what with Lady Awesome's book on self-confidence earlier on and now assertiveness training. I hadn't really thought about it much before but the various elements that had been raised were fascinating, yet so effectively simple when used in the right way.

We are all occasionally guilty of giving in on things just to avoid a confrontation, but I was beginning to realise that it had become a bit of a habit and I was now constantly apologising as if I had no right to exist. It was definitely time for that to stop.

My encounter with Magenta was also pestering away at me on the drive home. I couldn't get away from the fact that she had been talking a lot of sense. Writing a book was an achievement and so were my paintings. It was quite exciting to think that there might genuinely be a niche for them together. It was interesting that I had never felt remotely driven or passionate about my boring old office job in the last twenty years; I had saved all that emotion and intensity for my paintings and now my writing.

As I pulled Daisy onto the drive back at the house, I had to accept the fact that the answer to my future employment dilemma was staring me in the face. Particularly in the light of my sudden 'penny-dropping' realisation that keeping the book and paintings as separate entities made no sense at all. They were essentially about the same thing and thus legitimised each other in a very unique way. They were both very much a part of me and should be treated as such.

I guess in many ways, we mothers can get a bit fragmented over time as we morph into a number of different people for the disparate areas of our lives. We are perceived by others in relation to certain specific roles as perhaps a parent, a wife, an employee or an old friend; all individual compartments with precise requirements and expected associated behaviours. It's not surprising that after many years of this we can feel a bit disconnected from our true self; as if, in fact, our whole identity becomes a bundle of connected yet dislocated pieces and needs a little

Redemption

readjustment from time to time to remould it into a complete whole once more.

Deep in thought, I let myself into the house where it was immediately obvious from the cacophony coming from the kitchen that I was not alone.

Following the noise to its source, I peered cautiously around the kitchen door to see not only Beloved Husband but also the Barbarian Boys. They'd all successfully made it back from work and school and appeared to be engaged in some form of *Masterchef*-related activity. They do this from time to time. Beloved Husband is actually an extremely good cook and, on the rare occasion he dusts off these particular skills (other than for merely opening random tins of tomato soup of course), we are always in for a delicious dinner, which is just as well because it has to be good to make up for all the clearing up that follows. I am not joking; it can often last well into the next week. Great cuisine apparently cannot be created without every last saucepan in the house getting involved in the process.

I noted, thankfully, that he had already rounded up the boys to act as sous-chefs and they were busily engaged in peeling and chopping mountains of colourful veg. Quiet was tackling the onions and had carefully equipped himself with a pair swimming goggles, no doubt in an attempt to prevent the onion fumes from making his eyes water. Small had been tasked with peeling the carrots and was wearing a red and black spotted hankie tied over his hair and had a pirate's eye patch positioned over it to sit right in the middle of his forehead for reasons I couldn't fathom. (I've learned over the years that it's best not to ask.)

Alice May

As my equivalents of John Torode, Jamie Oliver and Ainsley Harriot seemed to have supper well under control, there was little danger of me being co-opted in to help out as well, so I figured it was safe for me to grab my laptop from the studio and join the whole convivially-creative culinary atmosphere. Setting up to one side of the breakfast bar where I could be sure of successfully sneaking tasty morsels without getting too close to any of the sharp knives being brandished about, I booted up the computer and opened my email account.

In the cosy, warm and noisy kitchen, a glass of white wine magically appeared in my field of vision as I mulled over the ideas that had been formulating that day. Sipping gratefully at a crisp sauvignon blanc, I pulled up a few specific emails that had arrived sporadically over the previous few months. They were from people I had never met. Don't worry though, they were not from over friendly, yet sadly dispossessed foreign dignitaries demanding that I help them get their money out of their failing nations by giving them my bank card details complete with security code, passport number, home address and my mother's maiden name. While I am not very computer-savvy, I am not daft enough to fall for that one. I also deleted the one informing me that I had won millions of dollars but asking would I please send through the very modest administration fee for the release of the funds.

No, these were messages from women who had read my book. I had no connection with any of them, so goodness only knows how they had heard about the book, but these ladies had experienced traumas of their own and they appreciated what we as a family had been through. In fact, one of them actually thanked me for my brutal honesty in

Redemption

telling my story. Others asked, 'What happened next?' and 'When is the next book coming out?" It would seem that there was actually a demand for a sequel. They were also keen to see the paintings I referred to in the book and so I wondered if perhaps this really was what I should think about pursuing.

Recalling how energised I had felt whilst writing each chapter made me realise that this was exactly what I'd like to do with my future if I could. It was the same sort of intense buzz I got with each painting. Perhaps my Barbarians had been right all along, this little unemployed interlude was just the opportunity I needed to consider how to move forward as both an author and an artist. Maybe the two together could be woven into a solid career. I wasn't quite sure how it would work as it was a little bit unusual, but the women entrepreneurs at today's meeting were all talking about the need to have a unique selling point. Maybe the art/author cross over was mine? It was certainly worth some further investigation.

"What are you doing so intently then?" asked Beloved Husband curiously. I looked over at him, enveloped as he was in a black apron with 'Britain's Best Barbeque Chef' emblazoned on it in bright red embroidery.

"I am wondering if I should think about starting my own business," I said with a grin.

"Really?" he said whilst attacking the contents of the wok on the hob enthusiastically with a pink plastic spatula. "That sounds fun. Tell me all."

That's one of the reasons I love him, he never seems to be remotely phased by any of the less than normal things I do; like coming down early in the morning to chuck PVA and tissue paper on enormous canvases or filling every spare corner of the house with random unfinished and half dry paintings. Even suddenly deciding to start a business, when I had no idea how to do it and no reason to think it might be successful, didn't seem to bother him in the slightest.

When I had started out on that crazy writing phase I told you about, totally out of the blue six months ago, and he had been scarcely able to separate me from my keyboard for more than five minutes at a time, he hadn't given the appearance of minding particularly. Although he did admit to me later on that he had been a bit worried that I might have finally lost the plot. Nevertheless, he had ultimately decided that the best thing to do was to let me get on with it, keep his fingers crossed, hope for the best and see what happened.

Now, when he could be forgiven for telling me to pull myself together and go out and apply for a proper job to assist with the family finances, he merely seemed genuinely interested in what I was thinking of doing. You don't get many fellas like that, so I should probably keep this one, don't you think?

"It would be a bit mad but I couldn't help thinking about it today," I clarified. "Unfortunately, there's unlikely to be enough of an income from it to begin with, but it does have potential." I told him all about my day and the thoughts that had occurred to me about melding my art with my writing into a creative business opportunity. I filled him in on the meeting I had been to and all the wonderfully inspiring

Redemption

women who were all so driven by a love of what they did that it was infectious.

"Well," he said, when I had rattled on until I ran out of steam, "there's no harm in doing a bit of research into it is there? You'll never know otherwise, will you? Can I make one observation though?"

"OK," I replied warily.

"I think you are missing a trick with all this."

"What's that then?"

"I think you should take your mother's suggestion about doing that talk for the Creative and Literary Society more seriously. Events like that would give you a platform to promote both your book and the art. An informal and relaxed chat with other creative people can't be that scary surely?" He was right of course, which is why it was so annoying.

"It's just so completely out of my comfort zone," I grumbled.

"That's no reason to discount it out of hand. If you seriously want to consider starting a business, then you should explore the potential opportunity that this represents. You will have to learn how to promote yourself. If it doesn't work out, then that is fine but you should definitely think about it." He smiled at me and raised his bottle of lager in a toast before saying, "In the meantime, here's to new opportunities."

Alice May

I nodded and raised my glass in reply with a grin. "Ok, I'll give it some thought. But it was just an idea; a little dream."

"There's absolutely nothing wrong with dreams; big or small," came the reply, "In fact, I might have one of my own!"

"Oh?" I asked in delight. "What's that then?"

He shrugged, "Yeah, it's nothing really but one of the senior guys at work mentioned that I ought to consider applying for this job that's coming up. It'll be quite a promotion though and loads more responsibility, so I probably won't get it."

"Well you won't if you don't apply." I said firmly, "I hope you are going to."

"I'm thinking about it."

"If this senior guy mentioned it to you then that's surely an open invitation to apply? They must think you would be a good fit. You have to go for it." I couldn't help but insist; he's quite brilliant and yet always so modest about his skills and accomplishments. Why is it always easier to encourage someone else to follow their dreams and yet we hesitate with our own?

"Maybe I will, maybe we both have a goal we should be reaching for," he said. "But right now, I am dreaming of stir fry chicken with black bean sauce, egg fried rice and some rather dodgy looking carrots. Any takers?" he demanded of the room in general, lifting the wok off the hob. The enthusiastic response from the boys was deafening.

Redemption

He was right (as usual!). There was nothing wrong with having a dream. Whether I could actually translate that into a reality was another thing entirely and the first step was probably to investigate possible platforms for marketing; platforms precisely like the one presented by the upcoming Creative and Literary Society talk.

There was no avoiding the situation. It was time to confront my nemesis head on; I was going to have to learn how to speak in public. Fortunately, Magenta had suggested we meet for a coffee the following week and she might be persuaded to give me some tips on how to go about it. I had a feeling I was going to need all the help I could get if I was going to succeed at this. As I looked up her email address so that I could send her a few possible dates I could hear that little internal voice of mine piping up, "And about time too!"

12. Germination

Definition: the process via which something comes into existence, the development of a seed.

*Staying with the **present** and the need to learn to speak in public….*

"You really need to get over yourself!"

Watching the steam rise from a decaf, skinny, flat white, I let those rather blunt words sink in. Magenta didn't mean any offence; she was merely being matter-of -act.

"If you are going to successfully speak in public," she continued, "you need to think about what message you are trying to get across. It's not about you. It's about what you are trying to say."

To tell the truth, I liked her 'call a spade a spade' approach. It was rather refreshing. I was here to learn and therefore her no-nonsense approach was perfect. There was no beating around the bush. She simply 'told it like it was', which meant we weren't wasting any time getting to the point over our drinks at the little coffee house in the town centre.

"If people are going to pay you to speak then you have to approach it in a professional way."

"Pay me?" I interjected, "are you saying that people would pay me to speak?"

Redemption

"Oh yes," she confirmed with a brisk nod. "If you do it properly and get onto the right speaking circuits. You could, in theory, get an appearance fee plus travel expenses."

"Wow, I never knew that. I don't think anyone is going to pay me right now. I will be speaking to the literary society for nothing."

"That's fine," she said. "You have to start somewhere. You can ask them to give you feedback too if you like. Either way though, you need to do a professional job or it's not fair on your audience. So, you can't get hung up on being embarrassed. You need to write a good speech, it needs to be entertaining and insightful with just the right amount of visuals to break the time up and keep people interested."

"No pressure then," I muttered.

"Think of the one person in that room that you need to get your message across to and focus on them."

"What do you mean?" I was puzzled.

"What do you hope to achieve with your presentation? Do you even have a message? If you just want to flog books then that's OK, but it would be better if you had a proper message."

"Obviously I'd like it to be entertaining but..."I thought about it for a moment before scrabbling around in my bag to bring out a few sheets of paper. These I held out to Magenta saying, "I want to tell my story for people like her."

She took the paper and scanned it. I watched as her eyes followed the line of text from one of the emails I had re-read the day before. It was from a lady whose house had burned to the ground a year or two earlier, leaving her in a terrible position. She had read a copy of my book had then written to me using the email address I'd included on the last page. She thanked me for writing about our story because reading it had made her feel less alone with the emotions she had experienced in the wake of her own home-loss tragedy, but it had also made her laugh too; something that she had found cathartic. It was a brief, yet powerful, thought-provoking communication from a woman who had stood in shoes just like mine and suffered in much the same way. If there was one person like her out there, then it stood to reason that there would be others.

"I don't want my presentation to be too intense or depressing," I continued. "It needs to be uplifting and positive because for most of the people in the audience it will merely be entertainment, but if I can connect with women like this one at the same time, then it might potentially do some good."

Magenta nodded thoughtfully as I tried to explain what I meant and when I ground to a halt she said, "Well that's certainly a pretty powerful incentive, but we'll need to get the tone right. Let's get down to business."

The next hour was incredibly exciting as Magenta and I threw ideas together, pulled them apart and put them back together again in various configurations to see how best to achieve my aim. My notebook was soon full of scribbled notes to follow up later, including tips and advice on how to proceed. I left the café later that day with Magenta's advice

Redemption

still ringing in my ears as I drove home to write the first draft of a presentation entitled 'Surviving the House that Sat Down'; a talk that was to bind together the events of the last few years with my two creative passions, art and writing. As Magenta had expressed so colourfully, I had a story to tell, it was high time I got out there and started telling it.

I could do this!

Couldn't I?

"Of course you can you daft woman!" My inner voice was back to berate me again. "You wrote that book, didn't you? That's something you never thought you could do; so why not this too? It's about time you found your voice and started using it."

"What if I freeze in front of everyone?" I whispered anxiously.

"Well there's one sure fire way to find out! It's not a difficult concept. You're a bright bunny, relatively speaking anyway, so get out there and jolly well get on with it! You won't know until you try." Having cast aspersions on my general intellect, the voice of my stroppy subconscious then melted away into nothing before I could think of a suitable response. (She's such a coward!) But I couldn't fault her reasoning. It was certainly worth having a go. What harm could it do?

All of these thoughts tumbled through my brain as I picked the Barbarian Boys up from school later that afternoon. Then it was back to earth for me with a bump as I slogged my way through a whole host of housework, gave what I hoped was helpful advice on homework, and cooked several tonnes of chips to go with a chicken curry I'd thrown together the night before. In between all these activities, I kept diving into the studio for a few spare minutes at a time to jot some more notes down. Eventually I was in a position to try the speech out loud in order to work out the basic timing of it. It was going to need a lot of practice.

Interestingly enough though, there was another meeting of the Brilliant Women in Business the following week and I had been sufficiently intrigued by my first encounter with the group to go along a second time. Now that I knew what to expect from the experience and didn't feel quite so out of my depth, I found myself relaxing and started to indulge in a little people watching as I munched my way contentedly through a pain au chocolat.

Lady Awesome was equally as dynamic and inspiring as she had been on the previous two occasions I had met her, and the group in general consisted of a wide variety of confident and motivated ladies. It was quite clear that amongst the coffee, croissants and chat there were some very fine analytical business minds around the table and yet this was not an aggressive Apprentice-style competitive event; merely a gathering of intelligent and capable women focused on camaraderie and collaboration. The overriding atmosphere was welcoming, relaxed and safe.

Those attending represented a whole range of ventures from small 'kitchen table' initiatives to large scale enterprises and they were interspersed with a few other women who, like me, seemed a little unsure as to why they were there but nevertheless seemed to be enjoying the experience. However, there was one particular lady who caught my interest. She had been a new arrival at the last

Redemption

meeting (just like me) and had seemed particularly nervous and unsure of herself. I was pleased to see that she had come along again too, but during the course of the meeting I noticed something interesting about her manner.

The meeting kicked off with everyone delivering a one minute 'elevator pitch' each like the last time. I'd been working on mine in the interim so was a bit more prepared than I had been before. It was an interesting exercise and really made me think about what I was trying to achieve and how to get that across to someone else in a short timeframe. I had probably looked a bit mad on the drive to the event that morning because I had been practicing my elevator pitch out loud on the way. The guy who pulled up in the sports car next to Daisy at one set of red traffic lights had given me a really funny look.

Anyway, back to my point. During this lady's elevator pitch, she spoke about making and selling organic ice cream. The group as a whole radiated a significant degree of positivity towards this idea, (after all who doesn't like ice cream?) but it wasn't a wishy washy 'oh that's a nice idea, dear' type of encouragement. Lady Awesome displayed a clear and genuine interest in the concept, coaxing more information from her about how she might go about it, and several other women asked pertinent questions about her proposed methods, sources and supplies before making some very useful suggestions.

In other words, there was no question that they were all taking her and her business idea seriously. The result was that the ice cream lady started to sit up a little straighter and speak with significantly more confidence. She had obviously done a fair bit of research into her topic of choice and you could see her passion for it as she raised a number of potential pitfalls and difficulties that she was concerned about. Other people around the table started to make suggestions and identify potential solutions for her, offering both help and advice. With this encouragement, I noticed that her language as she spoke about what she wanted to do began to change. She stopped using phrases like 'I don't know about', or 'I'm not sure how to' and 'I can't' and instead she started to say 'I can find out about', 'I need to learn to' and 'I can'! I knew I was witnessing something quite remarkable. It was like watching a new flower bloom for the first time in the warmth and light from the sun and I recognised then that there was a very unique power at work here. Together the group had created a subtle yet powerful shift in this lady's perception of herself and her idea, which in turn had encouraged her to believe in herself. A new organic ice cream company was one step closer to being born and I for one couldn't wait until I could buy (and try) her product.

Lady Awesome and her Brilliant Women in Business Group were a force to be reckoned with. Discussions about potential customer bases, stakeholders, communication strategies and finances followed, yet all the while part of my mind was marvelling at how the potential hurdles the ice cream lady believed were in her way could all be overcome. A clear route forward was emerging should she decide to take that first step, and with the right attitude, hard work and some effective encouragement and support I could see her realising her dream.

It was exactly what my family were trying to persuade me to do but my family know and love me and therefore it was hard not to brush praise from them aside as being biased.

Redemption

Bizarrely, it is more believable if a compliment comes from a stranger. Why is it so much easier to see gifts and potential in other people and yet constantly fail to recognise them in ourselves? Without self-belief we do not have the foundation we need from which to build our dreams and reach for the stars.

Slowly the pieces of my personal puzzle were starting to slot together, and a clear picture was emerging. I was getting so fed up with feeling inferior. Like the lady with the ice cream dream, I had a lot of skills and ideas too. It was time I gave myself the respect I deserved and started to take myself seriously. The aspiring child artist in me was still there and the long-held seed of inspiration, planted by my grandmother all those years ago, was finally ready to germinate and push upwards towards the light.

On the way home in the car I told myself defiantly, "I paint and I write and I am OK with that! I am learning to speak in public and I am going to stand up and be counted. I will tell my story. I will build an unconventional business for an unconventional person, an artist, an author and a speaker. Hopefully, other people will be OK with it too, but if they aren't, it doesn't matter.

This is what I do.

This is who I am.

This is me!"

"Hallelujah!" the voice in my head replied. "It's about time you worked that out. Now let's get this show on the road!"

PART 4

For my part I know nothing with any certainty, but the sight of the stars makes me dream.

Vincent Van Gogh 1853-1890

13. Evolution

Definition: **the process via which our early hominid ancestors developed into modern man**

*Let us return to the **past** and continue with that bizarre obsession with typing....*

"Did you actually come to bed at all last night?"

Beloved Husband's voice broke through my train of thoughts and made me jump out of my skin. I had obviously been really far away in my little fantasy world.

"Because it doesn't look as if you've moved at all." He continued with a grin and a lazy shrug, "Just an observation."

"I did come up for a bit, but I couldn't settle so I came back down. I hope I didn't disturb you. What time is it?" The early autumn mornings were getting so dark that it was impossible to guess what time it was, but the fact that Beloved Husband was dressed did indicate that I might have to think about morning related activities, namely the school run and then work (how boring!). Even though I wouldn't be working much longer, I had to keep going until the management transfer was complete if I wanted to get a reasonable reference and my full redundancy package.

"It's 7.30. I've just given the boys a nudge. They didn't like it much, but they should hopefully be emerging from their pits sometime soon. I've also made their packed lunches and now I'm off to work. Back later this afternoon hopefully."

"Ok, thanks. Have a nice day," I said turning back to the computer.

There was a brief pause in which he didn't move, and then he cleared his throat meaningfully. Looking back up at him in confusion, I saw him give me his mock-serious look and then say firmly, "Step away from the keyboard."

Puzzled, I asked, "Why?"

"You are going to have to do the school run."

"I know."

"In about 20 minutes."

"Yes, I know."

"Have you seen what you're wearing?"

Ah!

I looked down at myself and realised that during the course of my almost all-night typing session I must have periodically felt cold and, without any real cohesive thought, gone in search of additional warm garments. The result was a random selection of coverings each piled on top of the last, which could not be considered to have any degree of elegance whatsoever. In short, I was now in the centre of a round, padded mass of fleecy pyjamas, three different dressing gowns (only one of which was actually mine), a thick jumper, Beloved Husband's all weather gardening coat, as well as a scarf, a hat and a pair of pink, fluffy slippers.

Redemption

He was right, as usual (how annoying!), there was no way the Barbarians would let me take them to school dressed like that and, come to think of it, I really couldn't turn up at work in this get up either. It was time to stop obsessing with my typing and start being a responsible grown-up for a bit! I nodded sheepishly and saved up my document before logging out and heading for the shower.

Quite a few hours later, I logged back in having completed the school run, my shift at work and a quick trip to the supermarket for basic essentials. All the time my trolley trundled through the aisles of edibles, I was only partially engaged in the real world because a fictional scenario continued to play out in my head on my own personal, internal movie screen.

Once back at the house I was back in front of the keyboard again as soon as I'd put the shopping away, where I immediately resumed thumping away determinedly. Almost involuntarily, I systematically bashed out the specific details of the plot that had unfolded in my mind in the dairy food department. That led onto yet more developments and, even though I had my suspicions where this was going, I had decided not to fight it. I kept thinking that I would eventually run out of words and then this oddly literary anomaly would be done with. It was surely just an unexpected flash of confounding creativity which would eventually burn itself out and pass. In the meantime, I was quite enjoying myself.

It was something of a surprise, only a short time later, to see Beloved Husband wandering passed my studio window in the direction of the garage. He must have returned from work while I had been engrossed with my story. On checking the clock at the base of my screen, I was amazed to see that over two hours had passed and it was now nearly three in the afternoon. Minutes later he walked back in the other direction, this time carrying several large sheets of old cardboard.

I continued to type but with a degree of distraction now as I noted several more trips to and from the garage with a random selection of large pieces of junk being dragged round the front of the house to the side gate. Eventually I realised that Beloved Husband was definitely up to something and it would be wise to investigate what that something was. The estate agent had tactfully pointed out, only the day before, that the pile of discarded bits and pieces in the garage might be preventing potential buyers from appreciating the dimensions of the space available. (Why these people couldn't use their imaginations was beyond me.) Nevertheless, it would seem that Beloved Husband was now intent on sorting out the garage. This could only mean one thing. He intended to have a bonfire.

I suddenly remembered that I had hidden Skelly, wrapped up in that old bit of carpet, behind the pile of cricket equipment and other debris and thought I had better go and make sure that he didn't end up getting accidentally cremated. Hiding the family skeleton out of sight was one thing, lots of people do that, but unintentionally incinerating him was something else entirely. I was going to have to pick the boys up soon anyway, so having saved my document up quickly I then switched off the machine and headed outside, fully aware that once a bonfire was lit, Beloved Husband had the habit of chucking all sorts of useful items into the flames simply because they would burn well. It was an activity during which I knew from past experience he absolutely needed the supervision of another adult.

Redemption

I still had nightmares about one particular bonfire incident that occurred while we were living in the caravan in the garden after the house collapsed. If you recall, I mentioned that we had done our best to salvage much of our furniture from the rubble but quite a lot of it was damaged beyond repair. We had spent weeks redistributing various items of all shapes and sizes to other locations, storing that which we absolutely needed to keep and donating other reusable items to charity shops. We had also lost count of the number of tedious trips to the tip that had taken place to dispose of non-repairable or non-recyclable pieces. The remaining stuff ranged from large useless bits such as cracked doors from wardrobes that wouldn't fit in the car, through to smaller unrecognisable chunks of wood and these were all piled up at the bottom of the garden.

One clear crisp December morning, Beloved Husband had woken up in the caravan with the light of a 'mission' burning in his eyes. The warning signs were there before I had even poked my nose out from under the duvet. It had been a particularly chilly and restless night in spite of numerous hot water bottles and countless fleecy layers (including gloves and hats) as the temperature plummeted drastically. In an uncharacteristically early burst of energy he was up and out of bed, carelessly allowing a huge waft of freezing air to reach me under the duvet, hence I woke up too (the rat!) and before too many minutes had passed, he was warmly wrapped up and had also equipped himself with a thick outdoor coat and boots. Deciding that I should keep an eye on this suspicious behaviour so early in the morning, I hastily dressed and followed him out to see that he was stomping around the pile of smashed wood at the bottom of the garden, scrutinising it from all angles. I decided that a strong cup of tea was definitely required to get my brain working before I investigated any further and so I trotted off across the frost-encrusted grass towards the kitchen (the only bit of the house that was still standing) and put the kettle on.

In the time it took for me to make two cups of tea and head back outside, it would seem that Beloved Husband had decided to set light to the pile of wood. What is it about fellas and fire? Does lighting bonfires fill a deep evolutionary need? Perhaps the whispered memories of our Cro-Magnon ancestors still lurk deep down in the DNA of every modern man because there does seem to be a great deal of satisfaction to be had from kindling a blaze. Just as he was leaning in with a match to set the flame, I remember thinking to myself that he would never get it alight in the freezing conditions. How wrong I was! All of a sudden, a large flare leapt from the match in his hand onto the piled wood and a dancing circle of blue flames spread outwards along the ground in all directions. This flash of fire travelled at least two metres out from the centre of the pile of wood and completely engulfed where Beloved Husband was standing.

With a squeak of fear, I dropped the cups of tea and started running towards him, although what I was planning to do when I got there was beyond me. Fortunately, as quickly as the wall of moving flames had appeared they then disappeared, leaving Beloved Husband looking stunned but unhurt.

"What was that?" I demanded in shock.

He turned to me and shrugged sheepishly. His face looked incredibly odd, but I couldn't work out why. He didn't appear

Redemption

to be burnt at all which, given what I had just witnessed, was quite unbelievable.

I spotted the petrol can for the lawn mower lurking near the shed and quickly put two and two together making a big, fat, furious four.

"Did you cheat and put petrol on it to get it going?" I demanded crossly.

He refused to look me in the eye, glancing over to Skelly who was sitting on the swing nearby.

"Don't you dare blame the skeleton!" I hissed at him. "Did you or did you not put petrol on it?"

He hung his head and nodded guiltily in the general direction of his feet.

"Didn't you realise that in these cold conditions the petrol fumes would lurk at ground level and ignite rapidly like that? We're lucky you weren't injured. You could have set fire to the fence! Or the caravan. Or both! You great nitwit!"

My Beloved Great Nitwit simply nodded thoughtfully.

"Well I know that now, don't I?" he replied. "But look! It worked! It's going to be nice and warm here in a few minutes." He gestured towards the bonfire, which was burning away merrily now that the excess petrol fumes had burned off, as if that excused his dangerous actions. Giving me an incorrigible wink, he asked, "Any chance of a cup of tea?"

Growling with a confusing mixture of frustration about how irresponsible his actions had been and relief that there had been no permanent damage done, I returned to the patio to pick up the pieces of the two mugs I had dropped. As I passed the caravan, the door opened and the two boys piled out pulling thick coats on over their dressing gowns as they dashed across the grass towards the fire.

"Wow! Cool fire, Dad!" I heard Small proclaim, as he grabbed a long stick from the ground and started poking at the flames. I have long suspected that our youngest child possesses some of the very same pyromaniac tendencies as his father and therefore I was unbelievably relieved he hadn't witnessed the whole 'petrol fumes' incident, it would only give him ideas. Leaving my Beloved Nitwit Cro-Magnon Man Husband with the Barbarian Boys, I retreated, shaking my head in despair. Quite frankly, if the survival of the species via natural selection had relied solely on the fellas in our little family unit, then heaven help the human race.

Just as I stepped into the house, I overheard Quiet's voice carrying clearly down the garden in the still morning air.

"Woah! What happened to your eyebrows, Dad?"

Aha! That's why he looked so odd!

***

Back in the study, I smiled at the memory of that day. Nevertheless, I still felt it was prudent to make my way swiftly out to the back of the house to the garage to have a firm word with Beloved Husband on bonfire safety issues before I left to pick up the boys from school. Interestingly enough, Skelly wasn't where I had left him, rolled up in the rug behind the cricket equipment. Beloved Husband swore he'd not seen him but promised to be extra careful that he didn't inadvertently chuck him on the fire by mistake. The old bit of carpet was still there but not the bony contents, so it was anyone's guess as to where on earth the family skeleton might be lurking now. However, I couldn't spare the time to track him down right then. No doubt he would materialise at some suitably inconvenient time and place in the near future. I could only wonder where it would be this time.

14. Resilience

Definition: the ability of someone or something to recover from adversity or to return the original form after an impact

Staying with the obsessed writer in the past for a bit longer...

That night, the whole 'up-all-night-writing' thing happened again, only this time Beloved Husband came into my studio in the morning to find me slumped over my desk, fast asleep. I was in imminent danger of having the topography of my keyboard permanently embossed on my forehead when he gently shook me to wake me up. Sitting up in a startled daze, I wiped a patch of drool off my cheek. Then immediately remembering the last thing I had done before dropping off, I looked over towards the printer.

It was buried under a thick wad of freshly printed double-sided A4 sheets, some of which had spilled over, slipping down to cover the floor below like giant pieces of confetti. Pushing my chair back, I stood up and scooped them all together, sorted them into the right order and turned to him with a smile. "It's finished!" I said, giving a contented little sigh.

"What is?" he asked.

"My story."

"Does that mean you can stop typing now and go and get some proper sleep?"

Redemption

I nodded at him, shoving the pile of pages into his hand and moved towards the door. He looked at them with some consternation before asking, "What do you want me to do with this lot?"

I smiled sleepily at him, shrugged and said simply, "Read it."

As I was already on my way to the door, I didn't register the look of alarm that flitted briefly across his face. Had I not been so tired I would have realised that suggesting he read it was not that brilliant an idea. In the twenty-three years we'd been married, to date I'd only ever seen him read a grand total of about three books. Don't get me wrong, he can read, (of course he can!) but he just doesn't enjoy it particularly, so probably the last thing on the planet that he wanted to do was read my manuscript. Fortunately, I was too intent on getting some sleep to register his dismay as I staggered towards the stairs. It was a Sunday, thank goodness, which meant that I could sink into my lovely bed for a few hours and let my tired (but now mercifully empty) brain drift off into a deep and dreamless slumber.

***

I couldn't believe how much more human I felt only a couple of hours later, when I did eventually surface and clamber out of bed. Given half a chance, I would have gladly stayed there all day but sadly that wasn't going to happen. There was too much to do, especially when you consider how much time I had redirected from other household tasks in recent weeks in order to keep typing. Now all that was over I was going to have to catch up on a few more mundane matters.

Alice May

After a large cup of tea and a restorative bacon and egg bap, I leaned out of the back door to bash mud-encrusted rugby socks against the boot scraper. I have to confess that the beauty of the crisp winter's morning was somewhat lost on me as I repeated the action with the rugby shorts and then the shirts, smacking and thwacking the worst of the playing pitch off the fabric before stuffing them all into my poor old battered washing machine. While I felt sorry for the machine, I wasn't daft enough to risk leaving the dirty kit in a pile on the floor for too much longer. In my experience, dirty sports kit has a habit of reproducing exponentially if left to its own devices and I already had enough to contend with.

As I loaded the soap dispenser, I grumbled away to myself that Sundays were supposed to be a day of rest. Surely Sunday mornings were supposed to involve lazy lie-ins, hot coffee and the relaxed reading of newspapers from cover to cover? Although where I'd got this daft idea from I couldn't possibly say. It's not something that ever happens in this house, and it definitely wasn't going to today.

We had quite a busy schedule lined up and I had absolutely no idea where Beloved Husband was hiding. He seemed to have disappeared, but the boys had already started to ask me about lifts to and from their various 'plans' for the day. Plans that were going to generate yet more dirty sports kit. The only difference being that today we would be collecting mud from football pitches not rugby ones. (Sigh!) The rest of the day would involve a convoluted schedule of lifts to meet with or pick up mates to take to two different training grounds and then on to a couple of matches. None of these plans appeared to conveniently coincide on either times, places or people. This often happens when your teens have

Redemption

got carried away making elaborate arrangements over Facebook without consulting the unfortunate parent/driver.

If you associate with any young people in a 'responsible adult' capacity then you will be familiar with the type of day that requires a grown-up to drive the car in silence and wait around for undetermined periods of time in the cold, without actually speaking or trying to communicate with anyone at all. This is because adults, especially parents, are so *not cool* that they should do the decent thing and pretend that they don't actually exist. That was the sort of day that was ahead of me today. No wonder I was starting to feel a bit grumpy. My Sunday had the potential to be very cold and boring and, if I didn't manage to track Beloved Husband down, I was going to have to juggle it all by myself. I could refuse of course, but as the boys had been quite patient with me recently, what with all my obsessive typing, I felt that I owed them some dedicated parenting of some sort, even if it was only my ability to drive the car (and keep my trap shut) that they needed.

So, extricating myself from the evil clutches of the utility room, leaving the washing machine to chug away to itself, I checked that my Kindle was fully charged (in anticipation of many hours of hanging around) and then wandered over to see what the boys were up to. The PlayStation was in full swing with some sort of complicated split screen, multi-player football match taking place accompanied by running commentary and loud cheering. Clearly the boys were working hard on their warm-up for today's matches.

"Any idea where your dad is?" I asked.

Alice May

There was a long pause as each boy continued to press buttons and wiggle toggles on their handsets. The pause was so long in fact, that I began to wonder if I had accidentally forgotten to speak the words out loud. Perhaps I had merely whispered or only said it in my head? (As you know, I do talk to myself in my head, so such a scenario is entirely possible.) Just as I was about to repeat myself and this time make sure I used my vocal chords, Quiet took in a deep breath and said 'Uuuuuuh!' in a thoughtful way, which implied that I might get an answer, so I waited. Then he stopped, sighed and the pause began again.

It was time to deploy dastardly tactics. I shuffled round to stand in between the boys and the TV screen.

"Hey!"
"What are you doing?"
"Noooooooo!"
"You made me miss that goal!"

"Oh, good, you can speak! I thought for a minute you'd both lost your voices! That would have been a shame," I said as they tried to continue playing whilst peering around me. "Have you seen your dad?" I repeated, enunciating slowly and clearly with exaggerated patience.

Briefly, Quiet took his eyes of the screen and scanned around the room.

"Ummm. No, sorry!"

Small shook his head impatiently, leaned further to the right and fell off his chair as he tried to look past my leg.

Redemption

Realising that I was not going to get anything more out of them, I gave in and moved out of the way, setting off to track their father down. He couldn't have gone too far surely? His car was still on the drive and sparkling beautifully with the ice from this morning's heavy frost. Eventually, having looked in all of the bedrooms, the bathroom the dining room, the cubby hole we refer to as his study, the main kitchen/lounge once again and the under stair cupboard (in my defence, I was passing it and running out of options so I just thought I'd check!), I ventured outside to search the garage and the sheds. We own quite a number of sheds now as Beloved Husband has developed a habit of collecting them. I have wondered if it is a psychological reaction to that time when we had nowhere at all to put anything after the house fell down. We lost so many things in the actual collapse and were unable to store many of the precious items we pulled from the rubble and therefore we were forced to give them away. Perhaps that is why he has since amassed an impressive array of shed-type structures, just in case it ever happens again. In some respects, it's comforting to know I'm not the only paranoid wreck in the family.

However, we have got to the stage where I daren't let him go to B&Q unsupervised because I know he will find a reason to buy yet another wooden outbuilding of some description, if I am not there to firmly and repeatedly say 'No!'

Given the fact that we now have seven sheds, two bike stores, a lean-to log store and a little wooden cabin, it did take me a while to find out that he wasn't in any of them. Returning to the kitchen husbandless and completely frozen, I admitted defeat. I was totally mystified as to where he might be. Making the assumption that he must have somehow gone out earlier in an inspired (yet sneaky) attempt to avoid all Sunday related parental duties, I was forced to accepted ungraciously that the only taxi driver in the house today was me, so I'd better jolly well get on with it.

Stomping huffily off towards the stairs in order to find a sufficiently warm selection of clothing, of the type suitable for hanging around a series of sporting pitches and training grounds in midwinter, I spotted that my studio door was ever so slightly ajar. That was unusual! I always make a point of shutting it firmly last thing at night as part of my 'going round the house locking doors and turning off electrics' routine. (Remember the one that I said no-one else seems to bother with?)

On closer inspection, I realised that I had finally located my quarry. In the grand scheme of things, Beloved Husband doesn't usually go into my studio unattended, hence I had not included it in my intense search of the house, and yet there he was ensconced in the chair by my desk, with his headphones on, nodding away rhythmically to some soundtrack or other on his iPod. He appeared to be reading my manuscript, and by the looks of it he had been doing so for quite some time.

Interesting!

So that was where he'd been hiding. I tiptoed carefully away and carried on getting ready to go out with the boys. If he was going to read my book, then I was not going to disturb him.

Redemption

Just before we left for the first drop off on the list, I snuck back into the studio with a cup of tea and a plate of cookies and placed them on the desk next to Beloved Husband. A bit of a role reversal, I felt; me delivering sustenance to him in my studio. Admittedly the cookies weren't quite up to Chaos and Logic's standard but that didn't really undermine my good intentions. He didn't seem to notice so I crept out and left him to it.

During the course of the day I popped back to the house a couple times, mainly to try and thaw out between silent taxi trips. This was only possible when the training/match locations weren't so far away that I was forced to lurk unobtrusively on the side-lines remembering not to draw any undue attention to myself by accidentally cheering on my own child and therefore embarrassing him hugely. While home I took the opportunity to switch the damp, but now relatively clean, rugby kit across to the tumble drier in the garage and then fed the washing machine with the next load of dirty washing from the pile.

To my surprise, when I peeped into the studio, it didn't look as if Beloved Husband had moved at all, except to turn pages, as he was quite a bit further on in the manuscript. I took the opportunity to refresh his mug of tea and also provided a selection of sandwiches. It wouldn't do to interrupt his flow of thought with a rumbling tummy now, would it?

I had fully expected him to simply skim read it and then say something vague but relatively bland about it, but he looked like he was giving it serious attention. Obtusely, this had the effect of making me worry. What if he didn't like it? Was I making a complete fool of myself? I have heard it said that everyone thinks they can write a book, but it had never occurred to me that I might ever write one. However, having said that, it had never occurred to me that my house might fall down either, so quite clearly anything is possible as Logic is always telling me.

It felt as if this whole thing had come from nothing and yet the inspiration for it was no secret. Unacknowledged by me, all this time, my mind had been subconsciously replaying the events of the house collapse and the horrendous months following it over and over, to the point that the dark emotions generated by that time had to be discharged in some way. You cannot live well in a state of constantly high anxiety and there is no point in destroying the beauty of each new day by obsessing over what went wrong yesterday. Having expressed my distress, guilt and healing through my paintings, I was then in a position to tell the full story, to look at it all, in as unbiased a way as possible, aided by the clarity of vision that comes with time. To write it all down as fairly as possible and then move on. If I didn't, then surely I would keep repeating the loop endlessly in my head until I went completely mad.

Perhaps this book had been an attempt to regain some perspective over what had happened; to exert a bit of power over events that had been completely beyond my control. Maybe it was a search for some meaning in that which had made us feel so completely helpless. It was definitely an opportunity to have a bit of harmless fun, to allow my sense of humour free reign, and to make an effort to look at the whole event with an optimistic, light-hearted filter.

The incredible thing was that once I started looking for the positives, I was amazed at what I found. There were so many

Redemption

silver linings littered through our story. So many good things came from apparent disaster. Writing my story down had enabled me to see the redeeming features. Nothing is ever all bad. There is always some light in the darkness. For everything that is black there is some white too, and all the colours of the rainbow in between. There is beauty everywhere, you simply have to open your eyes and look for it. The house collapse was just an event that had happened. It was over. It had no power to hurt us anymore. By capturing it in words I could define it, put a full stop to it and I now felt ready to begin afresh and move forward with my life, stronger and hopefully wiser than before.

All the while that I chauffeured children around that Sunday afternoon I wondered what Beloved Husband thought of my manuscript. Would he like it? I kept telling myself that it didn't matter what he thought, it was only a bit of fun and, anyway, I liked it and that was what was important. I had to admit that I was lying to myself; I did care what he thought because as the day progressed I was getting more and more nervous. Finally, as the evening approached and my chauffeuring duties ended, I sidled up to my studio door and peered in. He was just reading the last page. As I watched, he gathered all the pages into a neat pile and placed them carefully on my desk.

I tentatively pushed the door open and looked at him. "What do you think?"

He scratched his head, a thoughtful expression on his face. Then he hummed and hawed a bit before saying in a somewhat surprised tone, "You know what? That's actually quite good."

Rather stunned, I was simultaneously torn between the utter relief that he liked it and trying not to be offended at how surprised he sounded about the fact that he liked it. But before I could comment he continued.

"I think you should consider sending it to some publishers to see what sort of a reaction you get."

Oh! He was serious!

My goodness! For some reason, I had not expected that.

15. Nascent
Definition: early indication of future potential

*Moving forward in time to **present** day and the approaching major public speaking event dilemma....*

The evening after my meeting with Magenta, I was digging around, head first, in the chest freezer in the garage, hoping to locate something I could cook for supper, when the landline rang. Abandoning my vain quest for comestibles, I hot-footed it back to the house in the certain knowledge that neither of the boys would bother to answer the shrill summons. They probably didn't even realise they were supposed to. As fully paid up members of the youth of today, they only communicate with their peers via text or social media and as such, a ringing landline would be beyond their comprehension.

Trotting hastily across the travertine tiles, I grabbed the handset rather breathlessly on at least the millionth ring. There was only one person I knew who had the patience to let the phone ring that long and the caller ID confirmed my suspicions. "Hi Dad!" I said in delight, "How are you?"

"Good thanks. Am I interrupting anything?"

"Nothing exciting. Just the never-ending task of attempting to feed teenage boys, but that can wait. What are you up to?"

"I'm just ringing to give you the heads-up on something."

"OK! That sounds ominous."

"Not really, it's just that your mother had a call from the Literary and Creative Society about that talk she told them you would do."

"Ah! Have they changed their minds?" Typical I thought, having dithered about doing it, now that I had decided to go for it, Murphy's Law would state that they no longer wanted me. "Well it did take me a while to get back to mum and agree to do it, so I wouldn't be surprised if they've found someone else to do it by now."

"Not exactly, they're still interested, very interested in fact, I just thought I ought to warn you that it might be a slightly bigger group than you were expecting."

"How big?" I already thought thirty to forty was quite big enough.

"Maybe eighty to a hundred."

"What?"

"Yes, there's been quite a lot of interest since the initial advert went out to members last week, and you know what your mother's like. She's told everyone. So, the Society committee members have decided to amalgamate the event with their annual summer fundraising dinner. The whole society will be there, with partners."

"You're joking!"

"Nope, I thought you'd want to know in advance. It shouldn't make any difference to your actual presentation but it's always a good idea to know your audience before you start. I go to lots of these sorts of events with one of my friends. He's a speaker and needs assistance with his IT equipment." That didn't surprise me as my dad is an absolute whizz with computers and is constantly being asked to help people out of technical traumas. "He always likes to know how big a crowd he's going to be talking to and what the dynamics are, so I found out for you. This will be a mixed gender group of mainly retired people. They'll all have had a glass or two of wine before you speak so they'll be nice and relaxed. I just thought I'd mention it because once you get over a certain size then the acoustics can be an issue."

"I see," I said, rather faintly. The acoustics were the least of my worries. I needed something to say first, but I could add it to my exponentially growing list of concerns. "Oh dear, I was just getting used to the idea of talking to a fairly small group Dad. I'm not sure I can do this."

"Don't be daft. Of course you can. You and your sisters never had any trouble talking when you were kids. Your poor brother could never get a word in edgewise. This is no different. You'll have no problem whatsoever. Now, I've been to events at the venue the Society are using, so I really rang to let you know that they have great audio-visual equipment. Computer, projector, mic and speakers are all state of the art. You'll be hooked up to a wireless clip-on microphone that feeds into a surround sound system. It's all really easy to use, but you must remember that there will be a small battery pack for the microphone that you will need to attach to your clothing. If you make sure you wear something with a waist band or a belt then you'll be fine, but be careful not to leave the microphone switched on when you're not giving your presentation. You don't want to pop to the bathroom and inadvertently broadcast your personal business to the whole room."

I absorbed this information in silence for a moment before replying.

"I'll bear that in mind Dad, but I'm more worried about whether I can speak at all, rather than if people can hear me," I said dryly. While my first instinct was to refuse to do the talk at all now, I was surprised to experience a small but definite seed of disappointment at the thought of pulling out. How interesting!

"You know what you need, don't you?'

"What?"

"A practice run. You need to give your presentation to a few smaller groups first. Get some feedback. Work out what bits make people laugh, that sort of thing. It'll give you a bit more confidence. Isn't there anyone in your neck of the woods you can ask?"

I realised that, as usual, my dad was offering very sound advice. It's one of the many things he's good at.

"Actually," I said perking up at the thought, "I think you might be onto something there. Thank you."

"Anytime," he laughed, "and remember two other pieces of practical advice when you are a public speaker; always take an extension lead with you to every event because the organiser will never be able to find one and the room you are speaking in will never have a power socket where you need one. Secondly, always turn your projector off as soon as you finish your talk, before you take questions, so that it can cool down. The bulbs cost a fortune to replace and will last longer if they are completely cold before you try to move the machine to pack it away. Other than that, you'll be fine."

It may sound daft but, as a self-confessed control freak, having some practical do's and don'ts to follow was really helpful for calming me down and my dad knew that. He'd obviously learned the hard way, from the many events he had assisted at, what did and didn't work on a more technical level. While the content of my presentation was up to me, the equipment I would be using to deliver it would be pretty much the same for any speaker and I needed to know that it wouldn't let me down. The only way to be truly confident about that was to follow his advice.

Grateful that he had warned me just how large an event it was going to be, I reconciled myself to the fact that I was definitely going to need to do a few trial runs before the big day. It was time to call in the cavalry. Having chatted for a bit longer with Dad and then eventually said goodbye, I flipped open my laptop to compose an email to Lady Awesome. If anyone knew of potential groups in the area that might be interested in allowing me to give a practice talk then you could bet your bottom dollar she would know who they were.

Half an hour later, while I was dishing mountains of my homemade 'special' fried rice into vast bowls for the starving horde, a reply pinged into my inbox. Lady Awesome had found a local Ladies Lunch Group who were interested in listening to my presentation and were prepared to give me some feedback. If the group enjoyed the experience then she was happy to consider recommending me to a few others, but she planned to attend the lunch group so that she could listen to my talk, just to make sure that she could make any future recommendations in good faith.

Given what an amazing speaker she was herself, I found it quite surreal to think that she was now going to come and listen to me. Torn between my default setting of automatic anxiety and a new burgeoning excitement, I spent the evening refining my ideas with regard to what I planned to say.

16. Incubation

Definition: maintaining an organism in conditions that promote development and growth.

*Continuing in the **present** and the lead up to the ladies lunch….*

Time was not in the mood to stand still it would seem, and the following week whizzed by in a bit of a blur.

However, by contrast, one thing was definitely in full focus during that time and it worried me far more than any speaking event could because I observed two more occasions when Quiet ambled back into the house in the (very) early morning.

I am the first to admit that I am notoriously nosy, but I couldn't demand to know where he had been without sounding like a Victorian parent and I knew from experience that this was not the way to handle him. He was clearly safe and not in any distress, and given his age I rather hoped he would eventually give me a clue as to what was going on. Any of the other Barbarians would have, of course, but I was dealing with the intensely closed-mouthed Quiet.

The situation bugged me on several levels because I knew he was going to bed in his own room; admittedly this was sometimes very late but, let's face facts, the teenage circadian rhythm does operate in a vastly different time frame to the rest of reality. I had even started checking on him in the middle of the night, like I used to when he was a baby, although this wasn't difficult given the way the fellas in this family snore fit to wake the dead. I didn't actually have to go into his bedroom; I could hear him from down the corridor. But I still had no idea when he was getting up and leaving the house, or why. I took to lurking on the landing at an earlier and earlier hour until I finally spotted him padding silently down the stairs into the kitchen. Peeping over the bannister, I watched as he made himself a cup of tea just before five am and then, steaming cuppa in hand, he let himself out of the patio doors and disappeared. Where on earth was he going?

I crept back under my duvet to consider this conundrum. Beloved Husband's advice, when I raised the mystery with him, was to leave well alone as Quiet seemed perfectly fine, but that was never going to work for a maternal control freak like me. I needed a plan of action; I just hadn't worked one out yet.

In the meantime, everything else seemed to carry on as normal, or as normal as things ever get round here. If I wasn't feeding or chauffeuring the Barbarian Boys around to school, sports or social activities, then I was writing and then re-writing sections of my presentation or boring anyone who came within three feet of me to death by forcing them to listen to it.

"Try to relax and enjoy it," advised Beloved Husband after my first few failed attempts to deliver the earlier drafts. "Don't try to be anything that you're not. This is your story and your artwork, so it really needs to be you talking, not some rigid, formal robot. People need to feel they can connect with you. You can use your hands, you know."

"But I thought I had to stay still so I don't cause a distraction," I wailed.

Redemption

"There's a big difference between having a totally infuriating twitch and merely relaxing and being you," he stated firmly. "I'm not suggesting you tap dance across the stage, but you can use hand gestures and move around a bit. Don't forget you have to fill the room, engage your audience. Get them to connect with you on a personal level." You might wonder why I was asking him for advice, but he gives presentations all the time in his job, so he does actually know what he's talking about.

"This is all so difficult," I grumbled.

"You're getting there, keep going, and for heaven's sake smile. If you look like you are heading for the executioner's block, you'll make your audience feel uncomfortable. I seriously doubt they're going to be throwing rotten tomatoes at you. Although I guess that will depend on the quality of the lunch as well as your speaking, won't it?" On that unhelpful note he gave me a cheeky grin before grabbing his mobile and making a hasty exit before I could throw something (anything) at *him*!

Eventually I realised that all three of my resident menfolk were actively avoiding me. The house was beginning to feel like the bridge of the Marie Celeste. You could practically see tumbleweed trundling through any room I entered as the other inhabitants retreated away from my approach, abandoning whatever they were doing to ensure their successful escape from being forced to listen to the latest version of my talk and then come up with constructive criticism.

Alice May

Eventually I rang my mother and delivered my entire presentation down the phone to her. All forty-five minutes of it. The whole thing was her fault after all, so I figured she should suffer with me. It didn't occur to me until much later on that she probably put the phone down on the side and let me ramble away to myself for a bit before retrieving it and making encouraging noises once I'd finished. I am probably being unfair because she did come up with some very constructive comments so she must have been listening to some of it, but it's what I would have done in her place so I wouldn't blame her even if she had snuck off.

Finally, confident that I had a sequence of material that would work to tell my story but also keep the attention of the audience for the required length of time, I then had to learn it. Not word for word, of course, but I needed to know the material so well that I would be able to deliver it in a calm relaxed manner rather than scrabbling around for words as I usually do if put on the spot for an opinion. I needed phrases and paragraphs that flowed well into each other and enabled me to express myself effectively, so I had to be very familiar with how the material should progress.

After that, I had to make sure I got the timing right. There was no point having great presentation material if I merely galloped through it with no sense of control or drama.

It wasn't very long before the day of the lunch club dawned and I found myself stood before twenty delightfully encouraging ladies who had just partaken of a deliciously wholesome quiche and salad (with no rotten tomatoes, only fresh ones – I checked) and were now indulging in coffee liqueurs and huge slabs of chocolate cake with cream whilst looking expectantly at me for entertainment. With the not

Redemption

inconsiderable weight of this group anticipation on me while the president of the club gave the introduction, my knees instantly turned to jelly, and I could feel my insides starting to quake.

Looking down at the prompt cards in my hands, I thought 'What on earth am I doing here?' as a wave of panic threatened to overwhelm me completely before my stroppy inner voice came sharply to my rescue.

"For goodness sake girl, pull yourself together! Just open your big gob and get on with it! These ladies haven't got all day." Supressing a small laugh at how ridiculous I would look if I started arguing with myself in public (been there, done that, wouldn't recommend it), I looked up at my audience and caught the eye of one particular lady sat towards the back of the room. She smiled broadly at me from beneath her shockingly pink hair and winked before mouthing the word "Message" at me. It was Magenta reminding me that this wasn't about me; it was about the story I wanted to share. Lady Awesome was sat next to her with an encouraging expression on her face as she waited patiently for me to find my voice.

Clearing my throat, I smiled at my audience and began to speak. My voice was a bit shaky to begin with, but as the minutes ticked by, I got caught up in the tale I was telling, the responsiveness of my delightful audience and the artwork I was displaying. Before long, I realised that the fear had evaporated.

***

Alice May

Later that evening, when Beloved Husband returned home from work, he came directly into the studio where I was adding huge curly black eyelashes to a rainbow coloured Jersey cow painting with a contented little flourish. Sitting on the edge of my desk he asked me how the lunch had gone.

"Pretty well, I think," I said smiling happily, "They were all really nice and gave me some very useful feedback."

"So, you weren't terrified?"

"Oh yes, I definitely was, but I got over it eventually."

"Sell any books?"

At his instigation, I'd ordered a dozen copies of my book to take to the lunch with me and I'd also made up a few dozen brightly coloured cards with prints from my paintings on them.

"Yes, all twelve sold, and I've taken orders for six more which is quite good. It felt really weird signing them for people. A good weird though. The cards were well received too. I thought I'd order some more bases and envelopes. Make up some more for next week."

"Next week?"

"There was a lady there who asked me to go to her book club next Wednesday evening; there are ten of them apparently, all willing to give me the practice and more feedback. Lady Awesome is going to recommend me to some other groups, and one of the local WIs needs a speaker to fill in at short notice on Friday. So I said I'd do that too."

"Wow, you don't hang about do you? Today a ladies' lunch club and tomorrow you'll be taking over the world!" he teased.

"Don't be silly! It was quite fun, but these smaller groups aren't the same as presenting to eighty people as an after dinner speaker. I need all the practice I can get."

"You'll be fine, don't worry. Remember, set up a file so you can keep a note of the figures from this though, like you do for your paintings. You'll need the usual stuff, income and expenditure, especially if you're ordering books off Amazon and materials for making cards up. You'll need to keep a careful set of accounts for your tax return at the end of the year."

"That's a good idea," I replied. "I meant to do that earlier but got rather distracted," I nodded at the colourful cow painting before me. "I'll sort it out, I promise."

17. Stymie
Definition: the hampering of progress

*Back to the **past**, the manuscript and yet another tedious house-viewing*

I closed the gate with a heavy sigh and leaned on it just to make absolutely certain that it was closed, and my unwelcome visitor could not get back on my property. For the first time in my life I could appreciate some people's desire to own a double-barrelled shotgun.

You've probably worked out that things had not gone well that morning. I had been planning to get to the Post Office in the village with my freshly printed manuscripts immediately after the school run, but my mobile had rung at eight thirty and a last minute appointment had been booked in for a potential buyer to see around the house at 9am. Apparently he was very insistent that he had to see the property today and that was the only time he could make. Somewhat resentfully I had to put my postal plans on hold.

Usually I would need more notice to tidy up for a viewing, but as the Barbarians miraculously hadn't actually trashed the place since the last viewing, I had agreed that a short notice appointment was acceptable. If only I was in possession of the gift of foresight and had refused, I could have saved myself so much negative emotion. Five minutes before the arranged arrival time, I had received a second phone call from a panicking Patience to tell me that she'd had a puncture and wouldn't be able to show the viewer around.

Redemption

The housing market was a bit odd at the time, not helped by recent political developments and the fact that it was now early November, so there weren't that many interested parties looking to buy houses just then. That detail, coupled with the fact that the cottage was rather a niche property given its size and location, meant that it made sense for me to show this potential buyer around rather than reschedule the appointment. Which didn't particularly worry me; it was a pleasantly warm, sunny day for the time of year and I was quite capable of showing people around even if I didn't particularly enjoy the process of watching strangers crawl all over my beautiful home.

For the most part, the viewers we had already shown around were really very pleasant people, generally families with young children or young couples looking to move to the country. Unfortunately though, when push came to shove, the sheer remoteness of true country life in comparison to town life was an issue. The absence of things like streetlights, pavements and takeaway delivery options were a bit of an issue. On the whole, people seemed to expect the peace, quiet and chocolate-box charm of country living but to still have all the conveniences of town life. It simply doesn't work like that, so our plans to sell were not moving along as quickly as we had hoped, and I was really beginning to wish (a little ungraciously I will admit) that people would do their research about what they really wanted before they bothered me.

One couple came out to view a grand total of five times bringing a motley collection of associated relatives. On each occasion they stayed well over an hour before they eventually admitted that they really wanted to live by the sea. Surely the fact that our home was a remote country property would have been fairly obvious to them from the start? I would have thought that the surrounding fields and woodland, coupled with the complete absence of sand and a large moving body of blue, salty water would have given that one away on the first viewing, surely? But apparently not!

However, the forty minutes prior to me very firmly closing the gate behind my latest visitor that morning had to have been the worst house viewing I had ever experienced. An ominously bad feeling had enveloped me from the moment I had set eyes on the squat, little man who had knocked impatiently on my front door. Although not terribly tall, he was of a fairly solid construction, and strutted into the house with a self-important swagger. My first impression was that he probably spent a lot of time at the gym given the vast array of muscular definition displayed by the very tight black T-shirt he had on (no sign of a coat even though it was quite chilly in spite of the sunshine). In fact, it rather looked as though his muscles had muscles, but I'm not sure if that is even possible.

With some difficulty I dragged my horrified gaze from his bizarrely distorted biceps. I can never understand why people do that to themselves; is it the pressure of social media or merely some form of obsessive-compulsive behaviour? It can't be easy not being able to put your arms down by the side of your body because your muscles are in the way.

Pulling myself together I launched into a general spiel about how the cottage used to be three hundred and fifty years old but that a significant portion had been rebuilt in recent years and was therefore of more modern construction. Not displaying any inclination to listen to me, he marched off

Redemption

through the house, opening doors and cupboards seemingly at random and firing blunt questions at me before belligerently belittling my answers.

The man seemed to want to argue with me on every single point. It would seem that I was incapable of being truthful about anything with regard to the house. I began to suspect that he might have a bit of a death wish, as my hackles became steadily raised and my hands clenched into involuntary fists in my pockets.

One major bone of contention surfaced when I mentioned that the property had its own private wastewater drainage system. You are probably well aware that this is a very common occurrence when you live in remote country locations due to the sheer distance from any larger residential areas. It doesn't make sense for the local councils to dig up vast stretches of road to lay underground sewer pipes all the way out to every tiny little hamlet where only one or two properties will benefit. Hence many country cottages like ours either have septic tanks or individual mini sewage treatment works installed. Happily, several years previously, we had installed a state-of-the-art version of one of the latter and were very proud of it. A nice young person from the drainage company visited twice a year to check it was working to the required standard and sign all the paperwork to comply with environmental controls.

If you've never had to think seriously about the practical disposal of wastewater from your property, then you really won't get how interesting the subject can be. Take my word for it. A person can get quite invested in such equipment when there is no other option available. Three years earlier, when the vast majority of the house had collapsed, it had been a massive comfort to us to know that we still had one flushing toilet. Admittedly, at the time, we hadn't been at all sure that the roof over that toilet was stable, but having an operational loo made everyday life in the tent so much more civilised.

Nevertheless, I digress! The presence of all the paperwork for the wastewater treatment system plus photographic evidence of its installation wasn't enough for this argumentative ape. He didn't believe me when I said there was no mains drainage option available to the property and kept insisting that he would get it installed, as if he had some sort of superior power and influence. I politely (through gritted teeth) pointed out that the nearest mains drainage connection was over five miles away and creating the connection he was suggesting would cost a crazy sum of money and require not only multiple and extremely complicated planning permissions but also major feats of inconceivable co-operation from both the local council, the water company and the highways agency. But he merely waved me away dismissively with that 'don't be a stupid little woman' way that some ignorant men have. I could feel my already raised hackles rising yet further as my inner voice muttered mutinously in my head, "Where on earth did Patience find such a knuckle-dragging Neanderthal?"

Quite frankly I couldn't agree with myself more for once, but I still had to get through the rest of the viewing without accidentally (or otherwise) knocking my visitor's teeth down his throat. I really didn't want to play this game anymore. Nevertheless, I took a deep breath and soldiered on.

What followed was a similar verbal exchange with regard to the property's gas supply. In other words, there isn't one.

Redemption

We use oil, but apparently Knuckles could get mains gas pipes installed as well as mains drainage. Good for him! Although I suppose if the council were persuaded to dig up half the county to put in sewage pipes for his sole benefit, then there's no reason why they couldn't lay gas pipes at the same time. Realistically speaking, there was no way that scenario was going to happen of course, but I saw no reason to argue with him any further. I had no intention of selling my home to this creep, but I did need him to leave without resorting to violence. (Let me be clear here, I was concerned about me being violent, not him. In spite of my unwelcome guest's sadly overdeveloped physique and bully boy, boorish ways I wasn't scared of him, just very annoyed.)

Then he launched into extensive and impossible plans to build a basement swimming pool complex under the entire house. Evidently, they are all the rage in London or so he claimed.

'Good luck with that one,' sighed my inner voice.

I did consider briefly acquainting him, yet again, with the fact that the property was within the New Forest National Park and therefore subject to the most stringent planning regulations, not to mention the complications of the Area of Outstanding Natural Beauty, Site of Special Scientific Interest and Ramsar Site statuses adorning the surrounding area too. A basement swimming pool complex simply wasn't going to be happening, but I decided that he could find that out for himself. Or not. Either way it wasn't going to be my problem.

In fact, by the time Knuckles had verbally torn apart my lovely thatched roof and then started to stalk around the garden, glowering aggressively at Beloved Husband's adored collection of outbuildings whilst looking for more things to carp about, I was starting to lose the will to live. Was he ever going to leave? Or even worse, was I going to spend the rest of my life chasing him round while he fired rude questions at me?

Trailing behind him at a safe distance, I watched as he yanked the door open to the log cabin where Beloved Husband keeps his (rarely used) gym equipment. I was surprised to see him suddenly stop short, his eyes momentarily locked on something inside. Then his face drained of all colour and he gave me a look of total incomprehension. He abruptly turned on his heel and headed for the side gate which leads to the front driveway, moving at a significant speed, where he got into his car, started it and drove away without another word.

Puzzled, but not unhappy at this sudden end to proceedings, I peered curiously in through the open door of the log cabin to see Skelly installed in all his super skinny splendour on Beloved Husband's old exercise bike; one of those more comfy constructions where you recline in a padded seat with your legs pedalling out in front of you and a screen at eye level showing you the mountains you could be cycling through, should you ever chose to cycle outside in the real world somewhere exotic like the Bahamas.

Skelly was sporting a luminous pink sweat band round his skull, a bright orange runner's singlet, complete with the number 13 printed on a square of white paper stapled to it, baggy yellow shorts and flowery flip flops on his bony feet. A small table had been carefully placed to his right, where a bottle of energy drink and a half-eaten Mars Bar lay within easy reach. He looked the perfect picture of the perils of too much exercise.

So that was where he'd got to.

18. Exposure

Definition: **the revelation of something secret, hidden or potentially embarrassing.**

*Still in the **past**, half an hour later on that morning...*

Shortly after the aborted house viewing, I shuffled into the Post Office with a large orange bag-for-life stuffed to the brim with neatly parcelled manuscripts. I joined the end of a fairly lengthy queue. Normally I wouldn't dream of going near the Post Office in the village on the first Monday morning of the month as it is always packed with people for some reason and the ensuing scrum is usually far too much for my claustrophobic tendencies, hence it's best avoided. However, my enthusiasm for my new writing project was sufficient to add steel to my nerves and so I braved the battleground.

It wasn't long before several other people arrived after I did, and the queue threatened to snake out of the door. Nevertheless, the lady standing immediately behind me appeared to be giving me a fairly wide birth because she was persistently refusing to close up the gap between us, in spite of polite prodding from the people behind her. It eventually dawned on me that she must have heard about the whole 'body in the car boot' scenario on the village grapevine. Her shifty behaviour made me wonder what she thought I was going to do; especially in a packed public place like the Post Office. Whip out a concealed weapon perhaps, or maybe just a blood covered body part? (I mean from a victim of course, not just one of my own body parts – although, come to think of it, either action would certainly liven things up!)

Redemption

Ignoring her hostile behaviour, I settled in to observe those queueing in front of me and soon realised we wouldn't be moving for a while because someone had just requested a 'check and send' on no fewer than five passport applications. Quite clearly a passport application novice if you ask me. No matter how helpful the ladies behind the counter in the village Post Office are, no one with any sense asks for that particular service first thing on a Monday morning? 'Check and sends' are definitely a quiet afternoon job, assuming that you don't want to be lynched by at least half a dozen people waiting to pick up their Giros, that is.

Nonetheless, even though it was going to be a while before we made any progress, everyone was doing that gentle rock from foot to foot that you do when queueing and attempting to edge infinitesimally forwards as if they could speed things up by sheer effort of will. Yet still the gap behind me didn't close up, not even fractionally. Thanks to the vastly over-exaggerated rumours of my bloodthirsty and murderous tendencies, I had plenty of room. Notoriety has unexpected benefits, I realised, because at least my parcels were in no danger of getting crushed.

The situation also meant that I could keep a certain amount of personal space between the rather tall gentleman in front of me and myself. He was well over six and a half feet in height and very solidly built. In comparison I came up to about his elbow, while the rest of him loomed overhead, casting me into deep shadow. This fact didn't particularly trouble me until his mobile phone rang and he dug around in the back pocket of his baggy jeans to retrieve it. Not a particularly remarkable action you might think, except that whilst pulling out his phone the loose blue shirt he was wearing over dark jeans rode up considerably and it became evident that he was one of those men who prefer to wear their trousers in an exceedingly low-slung fashion. So low in fact that I marvelled how on earth they were staying up at all. It was also sadly apparent that he'd had the misfortune to run out of underwear when he got dressed that morning, as I was confronted with an uninterrupted view of a significantly large portion of his very hairy and totally bare backside; a backside that, given his extreme height, was in lamentably close proximity to my face. (Do they not make trousers long enough to go all the way up when a person is over six foot?)

Mercifully, his shirt dropped back down quite quickly, and I was left doubting whether I had in fact seen that which I thought I had just seen; although the image was bouncing around the inside of my traumatised eyeballs like the flare from an unexpected camera flash for some time afterwards. Unhappily, this rude rump-revealer's mobile phone conversation was a brief one and he soon stowed the handset back in his jeans pocket, affording me with a confirmatory and crystal clear view of his almost entirely naked nether regions for a second time, and I was obliged to believe the evidence before my eyes even though it left me with an overwhelming urge to go home immediately and scrub my eyeballs with bleach. I couldn't help but sympathise with his poor mother; no doubt she would be mortified to know he had left the house with no knickers on. What if he was involved in an accident and had to go to hospital?

I instinctively started to edge backwards, unlike everyone else in the queue, while looking behind me to see if any other poor unfortunate had spotted this massive lapse in true British queuing etiquette. Surely it's common knowledge that you should at least arrive at the Post Office fully equipped with pants? The ladies behind me seemed oblivious, engaged as they were in a good old gossip which involved occasionally nodding archly in my direction. I was forced to conclude that criminally concealed corpses were very probably still the hot topic of the moment rather than blatant buttock brandishing.

The passports at the front of the queue were eventually checked, found to be lacking, and a gentle but firm lecture on what constitutes an appropriate passport photo delivered by the postmistress, resulting in the current customer at the counter turning to leave with a heavy sigh. One could almost see the air of dejected defeat hanging over her head like a little black cloud as she headed for the door with her deficient documents.

Eventually it was my associate with the well-aired rear end's turn to step up to the counter. I spotted immediately that his sheer vertical proportions were going to force him to have to lean down quite considerably in order to communicate effectively with the tiny lady behind the glass screen. It was clear that his shirt was definitely going to be insufficient to cover his stern in that position, so I closed my eyes and turned away. I really didn't need to see it again and there was no way I could effectively warn anyone about what was going to happen. A few seconds later there was an audible 'Mexican wave' of horrified gasps rippling along the queue behind me and then a shocked silence descended as numerous jaws simply hung open in a form of farcical, facial suspended animation.

Oblivious to the scandal he was causing, Mr Commando finished his transaction, stood upright again and departed from the shop leaving the counter free for me. Shaking myself free of a bizarre inertia, I stepped up to the counter with my bag of parcels. The surreal spell of silence that had bewitched the whole room was only broken when the door closed firmly behind 'the behind'.

Ten minutes later I stood out on the street again, secure in the knowledge that many copies of my manuscript were winging their way to sit in the slush piles of twenty different publishing companies. Feeling exhilarated at this small success, I considered popping into the village coffee shop for a celebratory cappuccino but on spotting a certain tall and low-slung-trouser-wearing gentleman at the till, I rapidly changed direction and wisely headed home instead.

All I could do after that was to wait and see what response I might get. It was going to be a fairly long wait. So long in fact that I gave up on the whole idea and eventually forgot about it, getting caught up in all the practicalities of the run-up to Christmas, practicing my synchronised swimming routine with the WI ladies and the final weeks of my nearly-over job.

Some weeks later on, there was a very interesting development indeed.

PART 5

'What we think, we become.'

Buddha 563/480 – 483/400 BCE

19. Self-Confidence

Definition: A feeling of certainty or trust that a person can have in one's own abilities.

*Moving forward in time, away from manuscripts and bare bottoms, to continue this tale in the **present** and the big presentation event that was looming….*

Several weeks of practice and preparation passed peacefully until it was only a matter of forty-eight hours before I was going to have to actually stand up before a vast number of the Creative and Literary Society members and speak. My mother had called to let me know that over one hundred and twenty tickets had been sold to the event and I was definitely getting very cold toes. It was one thing to give a presentation to a small group of ladies on a casual basis. It was something else entirely to be the entertainment for a large gathering of creative people who had all paid not insignificant sums of money for their evening.

It was all very well telling myself to pull myself together and jolly well get on with it but, as the event had got closer and closer, I had seriously started to worry. Nevertheless, I did my best to crush the mind-monkeys on my shoulder telling me that I couldn't do it, repeating clearly to myself over and over that I was going to give it my absolute best shot and all would be well.

I was secretly quite pleased with the way my presentation had developed over the last few weeks, thanks to all the constructive feedback from the various ladies' groups. The basic premise of the talk was to quickly outline what happened when the house started falling down and how we then found ourselves homeless apart from the tent in the garden. Then I planned to describe how we coped afterwards, as well as speaking about some of the very intense emotions which had eventually led to me creating all those frantic paintings and, ultimately, inspired me to write the book. I hoped that the whole presentation had a positive and empowering feel to it, based around the concept that it is possible to pick yourself up from the things in life which blind side us and that we can move on to a happier state.

On the whole, the practice events had generated some very positive responses and I hoped it would translate well to a much larger group. I also planned to illustrate the whole thing with original pieces of art too, and now I was scheduled to drive Daisy, packed with paintings, to Devon the next day. Once there, I would visit my parents for lunch and in the evening, I was to stand before the eminent members of the Society and deliver the promised presentation.

I had my timings all worked out. The required forty-five minutes was broken up into handy sections, alternating between telling elements of the story and showing paintings and describing how events had unfolded. Beloved Husband, the boy Barbarians and even the girls, on quick trips back from university, had spent quite some time helping me to establish a relatively professional delivery style. There were even several jokes, at least the Barbarians seemed to find them funny, unless it was merely hysterical laughter in the hope that I would go away and leave them alone. However, whether the Creative and Literary Society members would find them amusing remained to be seen.

Alice May

On the whole it was intended to be a light-hearted, entertaining yet ultimately inspirational performance. All I had to do now was actually deliver it without falling to pieces, a prospect I was contemplating with mounting concern as I dashed into town to do some essential banking jobs the day before I was due to leave for Devon.

After I finished my business at the bank, I started back across our little town towards the car. Whilst simultaneously stressing about the upcoming talk but also trying to keep myself calm about it, I took a short cut down a small alley where a chic little boutique was tucked away. The sort of place I never ever visit because I am simply far too intimidated to step through the door. I always tell myself that the clothes would be well beyond my budget and avert my eyes as I go past to avoid temptation.

Failing to avert them fast enough this morning, I suddenly found myself stopping dead just past the shop. I doubled back, to take a second look at the display in the window. There before me were the most divine pair of shoes I had ever seen. Now I have always appreciated the look and shape of shoes, but I rarely buy them because they generally have a 'too high' heel or 'too pointy' toe for my great plates of meat to feel even remotely comfortable. But these beauties had a graceful mid-height, spool heel and were decorated in bright blue with cheerful yellow sunflowers. They were totally mad but at the same time utterly gorgeous.

In only a few seconds I suddenly could appreciate what is meant by the phrase 'statement shoes' and the statement wasn't "Buy Me", although they definitely said that too. I realised that the longer I stared at them through the window, the more I was in severe danger of falling completely in love and actually drooling on the recently cleaned shop window. Yet, try as I might, I could not tear myself away.

I looked for a price tag in a vain hope that it would put me off. No such luck, even though the little white printed slip in the sole stated quite a significant sum. Not enormous by designer standards, after all we weren't talking Jimmy Choos here, but it was still way more than I would normally consider. However, there were some additions to the price tag, four incredible, little red letters.

S.
A.
L.
E.

Oh no!

Another lower figure was etched below the original amount. It was still quite high but not ridiculously so. There was nothing else for it; I was going to have to investigate further.

I checked furtively both left and right before reaching for the door handle. Why on earth I did that I don't know. Did I think that a police van would suddenly screech to a halt with sirens blaring? Perhaps half a dozen heavily armed officers would jump out and point guns at me and use a megaphone to yell, "Halt! Step away from the shoes!"

Tentatively opening the door as unobtrusively as possible, I slipped in and moved across to a small table where there were several samples of the most beautiful shoes on display.

They were all very colourful and hence so very appealing. I was beginning to develop a very deep desire to have new shoes, in spite of the fact that when I had left home that morning it had been the furthest thing from my mind.

Oh dear!

Dismissing the really high-heeled shoes at the back as unrealistic, I narrowed down my possible choice to three different styles, but it was going to be a very difficult decision. I tried to be sensible, taking the time to work out which of the outfits I already had in my wardrobe might work with each of the bright designs, and found myself coming to the unfortunate conclusion that I had absolutely nothing suitable to wear with the gorgeous blue shoes with the sunflowers on them. In spite of that fact, they were the ones I really wanted. In fact, I liked them so much I could feel myself generating reasons why I was going to have to treat myself to a whole new outfit in order to justify buying that particular pair of shoes.

Slipping them on, something incredible happened. They made me feel a million dollars. I'd never understood that phrase before, but standing there in that little boutique in those shoes I felt that I could conquer the world. I could certainly give a forty-five minute presentation, no problem!

I could do anything!

It was like a madness descending.

I needed those shoes.

Redemption

What on earth was I thinking? I had only just been to the bank and I'd seen my bank balance. It wasn't good. There was no way I could afford them, let alone a new outfit. This was absolutely not a good idea at all. But I couldn't help it. I simply had to have them. Out came my purse (entirely of its own accord, I do assure you) and I headed for the counter with an uncharacteristic, yet steely, determination in my step.

It seemed that at forty-six years old, arriving somewhat late to the whole shoe-addiction party, I was about to buy my first ever pair of fabulously funky designer footwear and it was an amazing sensation!

20. Incongruous
Definition: not fitting in with other aspects.

*Staying with the **present** and the trip to Devon for the presentation…..*

Twenty-four hours later my new shoes, packed carefully in tissue paper in their beautiful matching designer box, sat on the passenger seat next to me in Daisy while I set the satnav destination. I do actually know the way to my mum and dad's house but I was nervous and taking no chances. The Barbarian Boys had kindly assisted me in packing my little car full of original artwork, projector, screen, laptop, (I knew they had the necessary IT at the event but I was being over-cautious, as usual, and wanted my own equipment too, just in case) a collapsible table, a cash float and boxes of books, cards and prints.

Having done their duty by their nervous mum, the boys were now indulging in an epic battle of some sort whilst waiting for Beloved Husband. He had kindly offered to take them to school for me so that I could head off early and beat the rush hour traffic past the local town. But I knew that he had a big day ahead himself as the preliminary interviews for that job he'd mentioned were today. Hence, at that moment he was trying to get himself organised for the day ahead while the boys lurked by his car.

Watching them in my rear-view mirror as they pounced on each other on the driveway behind Daisy, I couldn't help but wonder why everything had to be quite so physical with boys. At that moment in time Quiet, wearing a long black cloak over his jeans and a sweatshirt, was forcefully bashing

Redemption

at his younger brother with the leftover cardboard inner tube from a used roll of wrapping paper and displaying far too much enthusiasm for his actions. While I thought it was nice to see him contributing to the family attempts to reuse and recycle things, I did wonder if I should step in and prevent him actively causing any real injury. Nevertheless, as the battle raged on, Small seemed to be fending off his brother's blows quite effectively with his own cardboard tube until, thanks to an unlucky mis-step, he was forced off the driveway towards the ditch. I watched my younger son desperately try to maintain his footing on the overgrown verge outside our property boundary. Instead of giving his brother some quarter at this point though, Quiet started hacking at Small's wrist and yelling:

"I
am
your
father!"

(Ah! That old chestnut! Obviously, he's not his father, but I *now* knew what they were doing! It was *role play*. They were acting! It was educational, how enterprising of them!)

Small dropped his cardboard tube and disappeared into the ditch screaming dramatically, "Nooooooooooooooooooo!" while Quiet swirled his black cloak around him and stalked off.

Goodness only knows what the neighbours would think of it all. However they were clearly recreating one of their favourite films. Star Wars in this case, or rather The Empire Strikes Back, when Darth Vader declares that he is Luke Skywalker's dad and then chops off his hand. They do this from time to time, especially when the PlayStation is out of action for whatever reason. I rather wish they'd choose some less violent scenes to recreate but have to accept that there's probably no fun in that.

As a mother I wasn't too worried by Small's current location in the ditch because I knew it wasn't that deep and we hadn't had any rain recently, so it was probably empty and there was no danger of him drowning. My only concern was the state that his school uniform would be in when he eventually climbed out and I briefly considered getting out of the car to haul him out to check it over but then decided against getting involved. Beloved Husband stepped out of the house and unlocked his car which caused Small to leap out of the ditch and race his brother (now minus the black cloak) to the front passenger door where a friendly scuffle over who was to ride shotgun ensued.

Beloved Husband raised his eyebrows at me and called out. "Go! You are supposed to be getting a jump start on the traffic. I can sort these ruffians out. Good luck and don't worry. Let us know how you get on."

Smiling, I waved at him and put Daisy into gear, pulling away from the scene of mayhem and considered how, contrary to all appearances, our Barbarian boys actually got on incredibly well as brothers but no-one watching would ever believe that. Neither of them could resist the urge to scrap with the other at the drop of a hat and I did sometimes wonder if that was normal.

I can still clearly remember the look on Quiet's face, over twelve years ago, when I had arrived home from the maternity hospital bearing a plastic, padded rock-a-tot car

Redemption

seat containing the latest (and last) little bundle of joy, dressed head to toe in yellow. We hadn't intentionally kept the gender of the new baby a secret but a very uncooperative foetus at all scans (a sign of things to come perhaps?) had resulted in none of us really having a clue if it would be a pink one or a blue one. It was my fourth time around, so I definitely had my suspicions but kept quiet as I didn't want to raise anyone's hopes either way. The minute we arrived home my four-year-old son had his eyes glued to the new yellow baby bundle with a rather desperate expression on his face.

"What is it?" His voice was barely louder than a whisper indicating just how badly he wanted the information. Do please remember that this was back in the days when he earned his (now rather incongruous) nickname 'Quiet' by rarely ever speaking at all.

"It's a baby, silly!" replied his older sister smartly. I forget which sister, which is a terrible admission for any mother to make but in my defence, I was only six hours post-delivery and hormones coupled with exhaustion had fried my brain.

Quiet merely closed his eyes.

"Please tell me it isn't another girl?" he begged with a disgusted sigh. It was a heartfelt plea if ever I heard one. So, I sat tentatively on the edge of the sofa next to him and placed the rock-a-tot carefully on the floor before us.

"Then let me introduce you to your little brother."

His eyes went round as he looked at me disbelievingly. Obviously, he had been bracing himself for the worst, but now he perked up and examined the little yellow scrap of humanity in the baby car seat with a bit more interest.

"He's a bit small!" He made this pronouncement doubtfully after an intense scrutiny and, in that moment, my second son gained his own, now completely contradictory, soubriquet. It doesn't take much in this family to get a nickname.

Given how relieved Quiet had been at the arrival of Small to even up the gender balance in our home, it was surprising just how many times over the years that the two boys have tried to generate benign physical damage to each other. I have made the assumption that this is merely a 'boy' thing and try to ignore it unless serious injury, death or destruction of property seems a probable outcome. At the same time, they have learned the hard way that I don't react well if there is blood involved, so they do try to avoid it. For the most part, I generally just send them outside to perpetrate their own personal brand of pandemonium where I don't have to witness it but today all I had to do was point Daisy in the general direction of Devon and leave them for their doting dad to sort out.

I had bigger fish to fry a little further along the coast.

21. Unwonted
Definition: unaccustomed, unusual or unprecedented

*Returning to the **past** and the wait for a response from a publisher...*

It was several weeks after my encounter with Mr Commando in the village Post Office that I was trundling contentedly past the autumn fields and hedges in Daisy and enjoying the low, late afternoon sunshine, looking forward to the prospect of getting home to a peaceful evening.

Having finished work an hour earlier, I had executed an efficient raid on the local supermarket before swinging by the Barbarian Boys' school to pick them up after rugby training. This was why Small, smothered in mud, was currently crow-barred into the back seat along with industrial-sized packs of all sorts of edible loot as well as enough rolls of loo paper to sink a battleship. I had taken great delight in packing several bags of fruit and vegetables around him, in the certain knowledge that this might be as close to them as he was ever going to get willingly, and that was only because he didn't want to have to walk the five miles home from school. Very sensibly, I carefully packed any sweet treats well out of his reach in the boot where they stood a chance of making it back to the house rather than being surreptitiously consumed en route.

Quiet, on the other hand, was sat in the front passenger seat juggling a number of mega-sized containers of milk loitering around his legs in the foot-well, with four multipacks of yoghurts piled on his lap whilst patiently listening to a litany of strict instructions from me to not allow any of the two-dozen eggs balanced on the top to get broken. All of a sudden, my nagging was rudely interrupted by a shiny, silver BMW roaring around a blind corner and forcing Daisy to veer right off the road.

Regrettably, such inconsiderate driving is not an uncommon occurrence on the local lanes these days, but at least one of us (I mean me of course) hadn't been travelling too fast and I was therefore able to skid skilfully into a handy, if muddy, gateway thus avoiding a messy accident.

"Woah!" said Small, "Did you see that BMW?"

"We could hardly have missed it!" muttered Quiet with his own signature brand of serenely soft sarcasm.

"I *did* miss it," I pointed out with some pride. "Quite expertly actually, but we were very luck this gateway was here or we could have landed in one of those." I nodded out of the window at the deep, murky water filled trenches on either side of our present location.

"That would not have been very good for the eggs," pointed out Quiet in a massive understatement.

Shaking my head in condemnation of the other driver's poor road skills, I coaxed poor Daisy into reverse, edged cautiously out of the muddy gateway and back onto the tarmac before shifting into first to continue forwards and around the corner, only to slow right down again almost immediately at the sight of one of those square, squat, refrigerated supermarket delivery lorries stranded in the road ahead; or, rather more accurately, *not* in the road ahead.

Redemption

Creeping closer, very slowly, we could see the vehicle was leaning at an awkward forty-five degree angle. The bulk of the main storage compartment was resting heavily against the hedge as the two offside wheels had slipped into the deep drainage ditch that was lurking beneath the undergrowth at the side of the road, no doubt with the express intention of swallowing up any unsuspecting suburban drivers.

It didn't take a genius to arrive at the conclusion that this vehicle was clearly another victim of the badly driven BMW. The poor driver had not had the fortune to be anywhere near to a handy gateway. It was pretty clear that the selfish speedster had blasted past forcing this poor delivery person to pull out of the way onto what he mistakenly thought was solid verge, only to find out that there was nothing solid about it and the results were before us for all to see.

"Ooops!" mumbled Quiet. "I bet his eggs are broken!"

"Do you think he's dead?" Small's helpful contribution came from the backseat in a dramatic whisper.

"Let's hope not," I said slowing the car down and coming to a complete stop right in the middle of the road (no way was I going anywhere near those ditches). "We'd better go and find out. Stick out the red triangle Small, back by the bend is probably best. I'll go check on the van driver."

Climbing out, I opened Daisy's rear door to help Small extricate both himself and the warning triangle from under the bags of shopping and left him to run down the road to set it up. Then I cautiously approached the van to peer in through the windscreen to see the driver hunched over the dashboard. He definitely wasn't dead because he appeared to be busy head-butting the steering wheel repeatedly and uttering profanities. This struck me as fairly odd behaviour but then I've never driven into a ditch; maybe this is standard practice.

Quiet, having carefully divested himself of eggs, yoghurts and milk, joined me next to the van with Small on his heels. He reached up to haul the cab door open asking, "Are you alright mate?"

The startled driver stopped his stream of rather fruity language and turned to look at us with a grimace, "Yeah! But I think I might be about to lose my job!" He laughed self-consciously before adding, "It's only my second day too!"

He appeared to me to be about twelve years old as he unfolded his long, lanky frame from the driving seat and swung himself to the ground. Obviously, he can't have been quite that young, but I would have put odds on him only recently having passed his driving test and that was nothing to do with the position his vehicle was currently in. He had the sort of frail emaciation that you see in some mid-to-late teenage boys when they are in the grip of a major growth spurt. You probably know some, when their height has outgrown their strength and their bones haven't yet been fleshed out with the muscle and general bulk that will eventually develop.

While I was making sure that this Lanky lad with the impressively varied vocabulary was not hurt, Quiet dangled his brother into the ditch by his feet (hopefully taking care to keep his head above the murky water) so that he could get a

Redemption

good look under the van and assess the damage. This probably sounds like a daft idea but, for a twelve-year old, Small knows a surprising amount about engines and general vehicle mechanics gleaned from many dedicated hours watching YouTube videos and has developed a worrying obsession with all things Top Gear related (more specifically the old series with JC in case you were wondering).

Eventually, Quiet hauled Small back out of the ditch having finished his assessment of the mechanical situation and my youngest Barbarian dusted himself down efficiently before declaring firmly that the underside of the van didn't appear to be damaged at all.

"We probably just need to pull it out really carefully," said Small earnestly to Lanky. "Then you can get it checked over back at your depot." Everyone turned and looked at poor Daisy and all reached the same conclusion fairly rapidly. Even if she was possessed of a towing hitch (which she wasn't), there was no way that Daisy was going to be able to come to the rescue. She was simply far too dainty. However, this was the country and we all know there are usually a high proportion of handy tractor drivers per head of rural population, so it couldn't be that difficult to find suitable assistance. Just as I was considering the logistics of trying to squeeze Lanky into the back of Daisy alongside Small to go looking for a tractor driver, there was the welcome sound of rumbling reverberating through the air, accompanied by a ground shaking tremor, as around the corner trundled an immense vehicle of precisely the type we required; the sort fitted with big bouncy wheels the size of double decker buses and a massive girth that seem to sweep right across the country carriageway from hedge to hedge leaving no room for anyone or anything else to pass. Perfect. Isn't it amazing how life can sometimes provide us with exactly what we need just when we need it?

Perched high above this impressive array of agricultural horsepower was one of the local farmer's many offspring who had no doubt been occupied in some late harvest-related activity in the area. From his lofty vantage point in the cab the driver appeared to be simultaneously chatting into a mobile phone held in one hand, whilst also eating an apple that was gripped in the other. One could only marvel at his multi-tasking abilities; after all talking, chewing and swallowing all at the same time isn't easy. However, I was more concerned with the fact that, as both hands were visibly occupied with other tasks, it wasn't terribly clear how he was steering the vast vehicle that was bearing down on us (but perhaps I didn't need to know). Our knight in shining agricultural machinery pulled to a stop within inches of Daisy's back bumper, tucked his phone into his shirt pocket and chucked his apple core into the hedge before dismounting from the cab and striding towards us with a big friendly grin on his face.

"Let me guess," this new arrival said nodding at the van. "Close encounter with a silver BMW?"

"Wow, how did you know?" said Small in an incredulous tone.

"He just tried to play chicken with me too, only I didn't lose. He landed in a field back there."

"Well, he forced me to veer off into a field though a gate too, so as long as he isn't hurt, it serves him right," I said with feeling.

Redemption

"Oh, he didn't go through a gateway, but never mind. I am sure the hedge will soon recover. I stopped to see if he wanted any help, but he was too busy swearing and kicking his car. I thought I'd give him a chance to calm down and left him to it. I'd much rather help you out. Is there much damage?"

Quiet shook his head, "None that we can see, it really just needs a bit of a tow to get it out."

"No worries, I can do that. Can you shift the little car? I'll get the van out in no time."

Dragging a very disappointed Small away from all the mechanical excitement, Quiet and I thanked him, wished Lanky every good luck and got back into Daisy to head for home and ten minutes later we pulled onto our drive.

Given all the extra excitement of the trip home, I was completely smashed (I mean tired – not drunk!) by the time we finally made it inside. Hence, I didn't immediately spot what was lurking in the pile of post on the doormat. I was so intent on unpacking the shopping and making a restorative cup of green tea that the mat and the mini mountain of mail on it were simply shoved to one side as we traipsed in and out with bags of supplies from the car. I then promptly forgot all about it in the commotion of putting the shopping away.

A large, thick, cream envelope sat, partially obscured by other letters, advertisements, a gardening catalogue and a plastic wrapped 'WI Life' magazine and waited patiently until I finally remembered the mail and went to collect it off the floor. That was when I spotted the unusual package and was very surprised to see that it was addressed to me. The only post I usually get consists of bank statements or the automatic TV license or car tax renewal letters, plus general circular stuff like adverts for pizza delivery firms and charity letters, that sort of thing. This was definitely not any of those. What on earth could it be?

It looked official. Worryingly official! Potentially something legal, perhaps? I employed my perfectly honed skills of procrastination for a while, first carefully putting my car keys and handbag away, before hanging up some coats and then tidying up the shoes that the boys had abandoned just inside the door. Then I moved all the other unremarkable pieces of mail and dealt with them, leaving the big envelope where it was on the floor by the door. I was simultaneously intrigued and perturbed by this item of post. I don't like the unknown and this mysterious missive represented exactly that to me.

Whatever could it be?

22. Recalcitrant

Definition: **having an obstinate and uncooperative attitude towards the expected way to behave under certain circumstances**

*Staying with the **past** and the intriguing bit of mail that has arrived....*

Eventually, I tentatively picked the large envelope up off the doormat and transferred it to the breakfast bar in the kitchen where I could keep an eye on it while I started to cook supper. It was still sitting there patiently an hour later when Beloved Husband came home. He'd taken a short detour past the station on his way back to meet Chaos off one of the trains, because she was visiting for the weekend, laden with the inevitable ton of dirty washing.

"Oooh!" he said, nodding at the envelope. "That looks exciting! What is it?"

I shrugged and muttered, "Don't know," in a small voice, just in case it could hear me.

"So, open it then. It's addressed to you."

"It looks official," commented Chaos peering over his shoulder. "I wonder what it is. Want me to open it for you?"

Beloved Husband, who is well aware that I can ignore the things I don't want to deal with for a very long time, picked it off the counter and put it in my hands. "Open it yourself," he said firmly. "Now!"

Alice May

Fumbling to get my thumbnail under the glued flap, I managed to rip across the top of the expensive envelope and drew out a dark blue glossy document wallet. There was a small window cut out of the front sheet of card that allowed the title of the document within to be read. My jaw nearly hit the floor as I read the following:

Publishing Contract!

Almost dropping the whole thing in shock, I looked at first Beloved Husband and then Chaos and tried to speak. There were no words, or rather more accurately, *I* had no words.

Chaos had plenty of them.

Her squeal of delight drew the boy Barbarians' attention briefly away from their electronic endeavours. They weren't daft though and only poked their noses through the door long enough to find out what was going on, before retreating to a safe distance. They recognised her tone from previous experiences with two excitable older sisters and fully appreciated that there was a significant danger that they might be accidentally hugged by an over-enthusiastic female relative if they got too close.

With shaking hands, I opened the wallet to find a hefty written document inside from a small, London-based publishing firm. Obviously one of those submissions I had sent out that day from the Post Office had reached their destination. Quite unbelievably, it would seem, this firm wanted my book! Wow!

As Chaos grabbed me by the arm and did a jubilant little jig of hyper-excitement, I smiled in a dazed fashion, all the while feeling oddly disconnected from proceedings. My stomach felt all fluttery and my legs went all wobbly and weak. This was a pretty sensational event, but contrarily I didn't quite know what to think. It definitely called for more than a cup of green tea though. Beloved Husband smiled at me across Chaos' enthusiastic chatter and opened the fridge to bring out a bottle of chilled Prosecco (it had been lurking there for ages, so it was about time we opened it). He gestured towards me with the bottle and raised questioning eyebrows and I smiled and nodded. As he popped the cork, the news slowly sank in to my befuddled brain and, by the time I took my first sip of refreshing bubbles, a goofy grin was starting to spread across my face accompanied by a pleasant tingly feeling that literally started to spread outwards from my core to my fingertips, enveloping my entire body in warm waves of cautious excitement.

Of course, sometime later that particular bubble burst when I sat down with the contract and read it from cover to cover, including the almost endless small print. Beloved Husband came into the studio just as I was placing the last pages down on my desk.

"I've done some research on the internet," he said, "and we can get some advice on the contract from the Society of Authors, apparently. Maybe find out the name of a recommended lawyer to check it over before you sign it. What do you think?"

"There's no need, I won't be signing it." I said firmly.

A beat or two of silence passed before he replied carefully, "OK! Whatever you think. Care to share why?"

"Sure," I riffled through the pages to find the one I wanted and handed it over to him. He read it thoughtfully, right the way to the bottom and I watched as understanding dawned.

"Fair enough," he said, nodding in agreement.

"There's no way I can sign that. It would be like signing away one of the children." In short, by signing the contract, I would effectively be signing over the book and all associated rights to the publishing company for very little return. They wanted all publishing rights, including translation rights in multiple languages, as well as film and TV rights and control of any related memorabilia (for which I read to mean my paintings), leaving virtually nothing to me whatsoever. The contract gave them the right to change my story too, as well as the right to never publish it at all if they chose to do so and they wouldn't have to give a reason.

My decision wasn't based around money; it was about governance. I didn't want these strangers having such complete control over my work. My story. I had lived every painful second of it and the resultant book told a tale that had been haunting me for months until I had finally been compelled to write it down. Now that I had done so, there was no way I was going to let anyone tell me what to do with it.

"Nice to get offered a contract of course, shame I can't sign it."

"Why not?" asked Chaos from the door way and Beloved Husband looked inquiringly at me. I nodded permission for him to hand the contract page over to her. It didn't take her long to read it. "Nah! I wouldn't sign that either."

Redemption

"Never mind," said Beloved Husband, "better luck next time."

I smiled at him but was distracted by the look on Chaos' face. "What are you thinking?" I asked her.

"Well," she said, breezily, "I think it's pretty obvious what you should do."

"What's that then?"

"OK, the very fact that they have offered you this contract pretty much proves that you have got something with this book, doesn't it? That it's a marketable entity."

"I suppose so, yes."

"Why don't you publish it yourself?"

Well that was easy enough to answer. "Because I don't know how," I laughed sheepishly.

There was a pause before she responded. "Yes, but I do."

Oh! How stupid of me! She was right! That was exactly what I should do. Why hadn't I thought of it before? Chaos had already self-published two books, so she knew exactly how to go about it. I sat up straighter, bubbles of excitement starting to fizz inside me. There were obviously pros and cons to self-publishing, but the major benefit to this plan of action would be that I would have complete and utter control over my work, from the detail in the story to the artwork on the cover. It would be completely and utterly mine, and the control freak in me really liked that concept.

"And you'll show me how to do it?"

"Duh! Of course!"

"OK, let's do it."

***

There were times in the coming weeks when I wished I hadn't started it all as the sheer complexity of the technical computer stuff involved dawned on me. My brain threatened to melt and pour out of my ears on several occasions as I tried to follow what Chaos was accomplishing through the self-publishing website. There were an awful lot of official forms that had to be filled in to complete the process, and a whole series of editing, proofing and quality control-type issues that needed to be sorted out before my book could come into existence. But it was also very exciting.

Then I needed a cover for it and spent an entire weekend dithering about which of my paintings should be used, before finally creating something suitable on Photoshop so that it could be uploaded and added to the written content that was already being processed as part of my project.

At last the day dawned when my book finally hit the online bookstore shelves and it felt amazing. The very first thing I did was to officially buy a copy and extravagantly arranged for an express delivery the next day. The poor postman must have wondered what on earth was going on because I don't usually pounce on him the minute he sets foot on the drive.

Redemption

(I mean that I don't *ever* pounce on him; I am really not like that, honest!)

I couldn't believe how surreal it felt to hold the first ever physical copy of my book in my hands. A book that I had written! The Barbarians laughed when they saw me immediately head for the patio in order to sit down with a cup of tea and read it; as if I didn't already know what was going to happen in it. I don't think they quite understood how special that moment was to me. I genuinely didn't expect anyone else to ever buy my book or read it. It was just supposed to be a bit of fun and I was pretty certain that I would be my only customer, but it didn't matter.

My book was in print.

It felt incredible!

23. Consolidation

Definition: **the combining of several elements into a single more effective and stronger whole entity**

*Coming forward in time again to the **present** day and the nervously prepared for big speaking event…..*

You will no doubt have heard the phrase 'silence is golden', but it occurred to me that there are many types of silence to be experienced in life. On the downside, there are the cold silences of hate and disapproval, or the painful silence of regret. Then there are many much more positive silences, such as that wonderful wordlessness that can denote happiness so intense that it cannot be expressed. Of course, any parent among us cannot forget the suspicious silence that arises from quiet children getting into mischief either.

So, with a wealth of silences to choose from, the silence around me just at that particular moment was a thick and rich one, packed full of anticipation. It was an ocean of silkily expectant silence with silver overtones that I was expected to dive into and fill.

This was the Creative and Literary Society's annual summer evening party where more than sixty couples were arranged around ten circular tables, draped with snowy white linen in a beautiful ballroom at a stunning hotel on the edge of the cliffs overlooking the sea. A delicious three-course meal (with no tomatoes!) had been consumed by all present, as had the contents of many bottles of wine. All that was needed now was a bit of entertainment to round the evening off in style and I was providing the entertainment, so no pressure then! This wasn't exactly the small and relaxed gathering my mother had originally proposed.

Standing in the silence near a projector and laptop arranged on a small table on the low stage at the front of the room, I could feel a tremor starting in my legs and reminded myself of Magenta's words of wisdom, "Don't be afraid of the silence, if the audience isn't silent then how can they be ready to listen?" This was the moment of reckoning. Here was the reason I had been working so hard to learn the many skills of speaking in public. Now was the time to find out just how good a student I had been.

I made myself look at the sea of still faces all turned eagerly towards me and absorbed the expectation. Feeling as if everything was happening in slow motion, a split second passed in which I acknowledged that this was the moment to panic if I was going to. Strangely though the panic never came, despite the fact that my brain was completely empty, because this wasn't the paralysing blankness of 'nothing'. Instead it was a space for absolute and complete focus. For the first time in my life I had something I wanted to say, and I was about to say it.

I took a deep steadying breath, smiled and said hello. I could hear my voice over the audio system as I launched into my opening phrases, slightly wobbly initially but soon settling into a calm and clear rhythm that filled the room with my words. Taking care to talk directly to my audience and not at them or above them, I spoke to all sections of the room in turn, making eye contact with individuals and drawing them into my tale as I produced original pieces of artwork to illustrate appropriate points.

The presentation I had prepared was simple and honest, and I spoke from the heart about the events that had inspired both the paintings and the book. As my mother had predicted, the audience were delightfully responsive and followed my words with a flurry of fascinated questions. I was almost sorry to find the President of the Society drawing the question and answer section that followed my presentation to a close. Almost sorry, but not completely so, because I had been on my feet for over an hour and was quite exhausted; if exhilarated at the same time. The whole presentation and the books and art had gone down a storm.

It would seem that as usual my mother was right. (But don't tell her I said so, or who knows what she'll sign me up for next!)

***

I headed for home the next day, after spending the night at mum and dad's, and pootled along the A35 in a happy haze of success. Sadly the speedometer did not once rise above a frustrating forty miles an hour thanks to a succession of roadworks. Thus by the time I arrived at the house, I was completely drained which was a combination of the days of stress leading up to the event followed by a very late night no doubt.

So, I was not really in the mood for a sudden phone call from the estate agent before I'd even switched off Daisy's engine. Oblivious to my state of mind, Patience politely asked if a viewing that was booked for later that afternoon (that I had totally forgotten about) could be pushed back from one o'clock to two thirty.

Redemption

Supressing a sigh and agreeing to the time change, I hauled my weary body out of the car, unlocked the front door and went inside planning a strong cup of tea followed by a swift tidy round. Chucking my keys on top of the piano in the hall as I passed it, I went into the kitchen only to stop short on the threshold, staring in confusion at the scene before me. What on earth had happened to my kitchen?

Never the tidiest room in the house to begin with, it was now completely unrecognisable. An unidentified white powder seemed to be coating everything, and everywhere I looked there were piles of shredded paper and tubs of slime. Chunks of what I could only describe as 'goo' clung to the walls, cupboards and door, and a trail of bits of old newspaper led off into the conservatory.

I stood there stunned, trying to compute what might have resulted in such a strange scene; perhaps we'd been visited by the Ghost Busters or some rather confused burglars? Perhaps the boys had decided to throw a bizarrely themed party or … what about……? No! I was completely stumped and had no idea what was going on. Then I became aware that I was not alone. Beloved Husband was peering sheepishly at me through the patio doors.

"You're back!" he said. (He's very good at stating the obvious.)

"I am!" I agreed. (I can state the obvious too.)

"It's a bit of a mess," he said. (He's a veritable master of the understatement.)

"Yes it is," I confirmed. (So am I.)

There was a pause before I continued, "Can I ask why?"

He scratched the back of his head. "Well, I thought it would be a good idea to encourage the boys to do something non-electronic."

"That sounds like a very good idea," I agreed, still not sure how such a concept might be linked to the total destruction of our kitchen, but I was willing to be enlightened so nodded encouragingly.

"I know you've been worrying about Quiet, what with him disappearing off in the early mornings, so I thought if we did something creative together he might feel like chatting about it."

"And did he?" I asked hopefully, thinking that perhaps all this wreckage was worth it.

"Did he what?"

"Did he chat?

"No."

"Oh!" How disappointing!

"You'll have to think of something else, sorry. But we did make a snowman," he said cheerfully.

"What?" Honestly after twenty-three years you'd think I'd get used to the way my husband's brain works but even

Redemption

after all that time, I am still pretty much in the dark. I was definitely losing track of the direction of this conversation.

"We made a snowman. Look! I just put him outside so I can start to clean up."

Sure enough, there in the garden was what looked like a four foot snowman.

"It's June! How on earth did you make a snowman?"

"Papier-mâché, of course." He said it like it was obvious. "I saw it on Blue Peter when I was a kid and I've always wanted to make one."

Looking around I realised that this activity did explain the suspicious white powder coating every surface; it must be flour and therefore not something from a dodgy drugs den. It also explained the piles of shredded paper and the tubs of slime. I could only assume that the chunks of 'stuff' I could see hanging off the walls, doors, ceiling and cupboards were escaped bits of papier-mâché that were superfluous to requirements. Beloved Husband followed my line of sight and coughed, "Yes, the boys did get a bit carried away. I hadn't realised that it was possible to have a papier-mâché snowball fight. They were kind enough to demonstrate. I did plan to clear it all up before you got back."

"Oh," I brightened, "so you remembered the viewing then?"

He paled, "Ah! That had actually slipped my mind. Oh heck, they're coming at one, aren't they?"

"It's been put back to two-thirty, so don't worry there's time. If the two of us get going, we can be ready. Bagsy you clean the kitchen though. I'll sort the bedrooms out." I grinned, knowing I was getting the better deal. To be fair it was usually me causing creative chaos, it was nice that someone else had indulged for a change.

***

Several hours later, following an extensive application of elbow grease, the house looked so much better.

Beloved Husband met me at the bottom of the stairs as I was coming down laden with dirty washing. Still sporting a streak of flour through his hair, he hefted the huge bundle off me and asked, "Where do you want this? Utility room?"

"Can you stick it in the back of your car?" I asked.

He looked at me askance. "Why?"

"Because I want to hide it, not wash it. I was going to put it in Daisy like I usually do, but she's full of paintings. I haven't had a chance to unload her yet. I'll do it after the viewing." I followed him out to the car to open the boot for him, so I could keep talking, "I'm really starting to hate these viewings you know. Hopefully this lot will be better than the last one. He was mental. It's such a shame we can't just take the house off the market and stay here forever."

"Well perhaps we should think about it," Beloved Husband said with a shrug.

Redemption

"We can't afford it," was my blunt reply. "Remember Mortimer?"

"Yes, but the only offers we've had have been way below the asking price and we can't afford to accept those, can we? Time is passing and yet somehow we do seem to be managing each month to make the mortgage repayments. Perhaps we should consider trying to ride it out. And don't forget, if I get that promotion it'll mean quite a jump in salary."

"Well, I know you're on the shortlist which is great, but there's still the final interview to go, and I'm still unemployed so let's just wait and see. In the meantime, now the housework is sorted, why don't you take me out for a coffee while Patience does the whole patience routine with these viewers?"

"Sounds like a plan," he said, "and then you can tell me how your presentation went."

"Deal, but first we have to remember to hide Skelly so he doesn't frighten off this lot of viewers. Have you any idea where he is right now?"

"Yup, Skelly went into school this morning with the boys, so he's not a problem we have to worry about today." Beloved Husband managed to get that whole sentence out with a completely straight face too. Incredible!

"Dare I ask why?" I said, not really sure that I wanted to know.

"Biology, show and tell, I think. Don't worry! He went in wearing full school uniform. Small even packed him a lunch."

I thought it best to leave the subject there, but I did wonder what the Headmaster would make of our smallest Barbarian dragging the family skeleton around with him at school all day.

Only time would tell.

24. Potential

Definition: latent qualities that might develop into future success.

*Staying with the **present** and that celebratory cup of coffee I mentioned...*

"I never thought I would say this, but I really enjoyed it." I said, once my hands were wrapped around a decaff, skinny cappuccino in the cute little coffee shop squeezed between the village shop and the Post Office.

The shop was absolutely heaving with local mums having a last- minute cuppa before heading for the local primary school playground for pick up. We had been very lucky to get a seat at all, let alone prime position by the window where we could see across the village green and watch the various comings and goings to our heart's content whilst commenting idly on recent events.

"I thought you would, when you got going. It's a good presentation and you can be quite funny when you relax."

I stared at him. "Funny 'good' or funny 'weird'?"

He paused for a moment and wrinkled his nose at me before saying wickedly, "Definitely funny weird, of course," and then ducked as I threw the little biscuit lurking in my saucer at him.

Catching it deftly he popped it in his mouth, and chewed and swallowed it in seconds, "Yum! Thanks!"

"And I got so many comments on my funky new shoes!"

He looked at me doubtfully, "Seriously?"

"Yes!" I insisted. "You're a man, you wouldn't understand it, but so many of the women there complimented me on my shoes. It really helped to break the ice on a social level. You know I'm not the best at mingling with a bunch of strangers but the shoes provided a talking point. There isn't a woman alive who doesn't like shoes? Hence there's an immediate connection. Plus, I could stand all night in them and they didn't hurt."

The expression of total bewilderment on his face at that point was an absolute picture.

"Honestly, they were such a good investment!" I declared.

"Yeah, you keep telling yourself that," he said with a grin. "More importantly, did you sell any books?"

"I did, yes. I sold out."

"No way! I thought you took three boxes?"

"I did. I just kept signing them until a lady asked me if I had any more and when I said 'yes, look in the other box', she said 'I have, it's empty' which was when I realised I'd run out."

Reaching over, I nicked the mini biscuit sitting on his saucer and chomped on it.

Redemption

"That's a shame. Not a shame you sold them all, just that you could have sold more."

"Aha! But I did sell more," I exclaimed happily. "I just took a list of names and addresses and they paid me the cost of the book in advance, plus a bit extra for postage. I am going to place an order this afternoon and then when it arrives, I'll sign them all and post them off to their new owners."

"Seriously? Well done for thinking on your feet!"

"It was the shoes," I quipped. "I told you they were a good investment. I sold loads of cards too."

"I am not surprised about that," he said. "They are nice and bright and quite unusual. Also, they're a good memento of a fun evening, I should imagine."

"And each one advertises my book on the back too, so I might get a few more sales off that as well. I also got chatting to a really nice woman from a mental health charity. She was really interested in the concept of the paintings telling the story of my recovery from depression. She mentioned that there was a big fundraiser coming up and when I offered to donate a painting for the raffle, she asked me if I would consider speaking for them."

"That's a good idea. So, all in all would you say it was a fairly successful event?"

"I haven't got to the best bit yet," I said.

"Well don't keep me in suspense."

"I sold *two* paintings. Big ones."

"But I thought you put quite high prices on them."

"I did. But the buyers didn't bat an eyelid at the amount. They just handed over cheques and took the paintings home with them at the end of the evening. I probably should have waited for the cheques to clear before releasing the paintings because they could bounce, but I don't think they will. "

He gave a low whistle. "If you keep that up we really can take the house off the market, you know."

I shook my head at him seriously, "I don't think so. It was probably all a bit of a fluke, but it was a really fun evening nevertheless, and I wouldn't mind doing that sort of thing again if I get the opportunity, but it's unlikely to happen."

"Don't underestimate yourself, let's just see what happens."

"OK," I nodded in agreement and then changed the subject. "Now, what are we going to do about Quiet?"

"Ah! I was thinking about that while I was scraping papier-mâché off the ceiling" he said and leaned in towards me, "I have a cunning plan!"

Given that his last idea involved creating a four-foot snowman using flour, water and a torn up copy of the Yellow Pages, I couldn't wait to hear what he'd come up with this time.

Part 6

'There is nothing impossible to him who will try.'

Alexander the Great 356BC 323BC

25. Prorogation

Definition: a period of time between the ending of one thing and the beginning of another

*Let us travel one final time into the **past**, to see what happened after the official publication of the book...*

Several changes occurred in the next few weeks following the publication of my book. Christmas was over, as was the old year, and the final weeks of my job were complete. My twenty-year status as a gainfully employed person was over and I was set adrift on the ocean of redundancy.

You have probably noticed by now that I do not handle change terribly well and this was no different. Instead of doing something practical about it, like looking for another job, I ignored the situation and buried myself in my studio. With no overwhelming urge to write taking predominance, I returned to my first love. Painting!

It must be borne in mind that the house was still on the market, so I had to try to paint tidily, which was proving a challenge but not stopping me. After four months of sporadic viewings, one might wonder why there had been no sign of a sale but there were any number of reasons why that might have been; from the wrong time of the year, a generally poor housing market or post-Brexit issues. Plus, the house was in a very remote area and, on the whole, most people want the practicality and convenience of a more urban environment. As you might expect, we had been in receipt of the usual offensively low offers from people chancing their arm, but nothing that had made any financial sense to us, so these had been given short shrift. The upshot

Redemption

of all that was that we were still trying to exist in an unnaturally (for us) organised and neat way, or at least I was. I could be pretty certain that the boys weren't trying too hard to be tidy judging from the state of their bedrooms. Unfortunately, there is only so much stuff you can ram under the bed or behind the wardrobe, and we were reaching the stage where a major reshuffle or 'spring clean' was going to be needed. You could say that this might be a better way to occupy my newly-redundant time, but I merely told myself it wasn't quite Spring yet, closed my studio door to it all and opened tubes of paint instead.

The result was a series of small, brightly coloured random animal pictures; a field mouse, a trio of gossiping giraffes, an elephant or two and a happy looking hippo. These creations helped the icy cold months of January and February to slowly slide past.

It was during that time that two developments became apparent to me. The first was that my youngest son had definitely lost the ability to hang up wet towels, which I believe is a stage that all teenage boys reach at some point or another, usually around the time their parents start repeatedly insisting that daily showers and hair washes are an absolute necessity. One morning, totally stumped by the mysterious disappearance of every towel in the house, from my posh Egyptian cottons (they were a present ages ago and only used on special occasions) to our usual Tesco's basics. I was forced to investigate Small's bedroom where I was to discover that he had amassed an impressively festering collection of bath sheets over several weeks.

Retrieving the manky, mouldy mound of fluffy fabric from under the bed and heading for the utility room, I walked past the front door to see that the postman had been. There was a littering of letters lounging nonchalantly on the mat. Setting the washer going on what was to be the first of many washes with my fingers crossed that the ancient apparatus would cope with all the towels, I wandered back to retrieve the post.

This was when the second development I mentioned manifested itself with the suspicion that my mother was up to something. One of the items of mail was a very pretty pink envelope addressed to me from my sister's godmother. (No, I am not psychic! There was a little return address sticker attached to the back of it; the type that sensible, organised and properly grown-up people use. I might even get some, one day.) Now I adore my youngest sister's godmother, she is wonderful, but she and I are not in the habit of exchanging snail mail on a regular basis, so something was definitely afoot. As I mentioned previously, I rarely get proper mail so I was intrigued and hence I opened it carefully and with relish. A proper old fashioned, written communiqué is something to be enjoyed and treated with respect, don't you think? Inside was a gorgeous, flowered piece of writing paper covered in traditionally cursive script. Reading the beautifully written sentences it contained, I smiled and reached for the telephone, dialled quickly and perched myself comfortably on a stool at the breakfast bar in the kitchen as I listened to the resulting dialling tone. As soon as the call was picked up, I got straight to the point.

"What are you up to, Mum?"

There was a pause before she replied, "Me? I don't know what you mean!" There was an air of mystified innocence behind the smile in her voice, but I wasn't fooled.

"Ok," I agreed, playing along, "Then perhaps you can tell me why I've just received a really lovely letter from one of your very good friends saying how much they enjoyed reading my book?"

"Oh, how nice!" she sounded absolutely delighted, "Your first piece of proper fan mail. Who was that from then?"

"Hardly fan mail, Mum. But who on earth do you think it's from? I assume you must have given her a copy."

"Oh yes I probably did, but…." she sounded genuinely mystified, "I couldn't possibly guess who might have written to you."

"Well how many copies have you given to people then?" I asked in surprise.

"Hundreds!" interrupted my Dad's voice. He'd obviously heard the phone ring, worked out it was me and picked up the second handset upstairs so he could join in the conversation. "She's sent so many copies out to her friends that I've lost count!"

"Seriously?"

"Don't exaggerate!" Mum said in an exasperated voice. "I've only sent out a few. Although I have given some as presents recently, and I mentioned it to the ladies at my dance, keep fit and yoga classes. Then your dad's mentioned it at his French conversation group, the Twinning Association, the sailing club and the Rotary Club. So I suppose there are quite a few people it might be."

"Why?" I asked, rather stunned.

She laughed, "Why do you think, you daft girl? We enjoyed it and thought they might like to read it too. Isn't that why you published it?"

"I suppose so. I just didn't really think anyone would want to read it."

"Have you looked on Amazon recently?" That was my dad again. "You've got some reviews! Four and five star reviews."

"No way!" I exclaimed in amazement.

"Yes, have a look!"

"That's unbelievable. Hang on let me pull up the website and see what it says." I flipped open the iPad and quickly Googled both Amazon and the self-publishing website to see reviews and any recent book sales activity. As I hadn't expected anyone to buy it and wasn't promoting it like you are supposed to on all social media forums (I didn't really know how to, even though Chaos had tried to show me), I hadn't bothered to look at the sales report page before now.

"Wow! Mum! How many copies did you buy?" I asked incredulously when I saw the report.

"Yes, how many did you buy?" echoed my dad with a more suspicious tone.

Redemption

"Oh not that many, maybe ten….possibly twelve… or so… I forget. They were just a few presents for people, that sort of thing, you know how it is," she tailed off, vaguely. I wasn't fooled though, she's as sharp as a tack and I've used the same ambiguous tactic myself to deflect my own husband's queries with regard to my spending habits. Who do you think I learned it from?

Looking at the website I could see far more activity than a dozen book sales, but there was no way she could have bought them all. The sales graph showed a healthy selection of spikes of increasing significance over the last few weeks.

Then I opened another tab to look up those reviews Dad mentioned, and he was right. Several four and five star reviews were listed under the page for my book. There was a one star review too but that didn't faze me. Show me an author who hasn't had a one star review. It's practically a rite of passage and you can't please everyone. All the other comments were really positive. How amazing!

"Well that's interesting." I said, "I probably ought to dig out the bit of paper I wrote Chaos' marketing instructions down on and try a bit of advertising."

"Ah!" Something about my mother's tone got my attention from the reviews on the screen in front of me.

"Mum?" I queried. "What else is going on?"

"I take it that you haven't been on Facebook recently then."

"When have I ever been on Facebook? I know Chaos set me up an account with an author page, but I haven't really bothered with it. I had no idea what I was supposed to write on it."

"Oh, don't worry! She's been doing that for you. At least I think it's her."

"She's supposed to be studying." I said, repressively.

"I am sure she is, but no doubt she is able to multi-screen as well as the next student and who else is it likely to be? There have been some very exciting posts on your page. Apparently you're going on a book tour."

"I'm what? When? Where?"

Dad broke back into the conversation to say sensibly, "I think you probably ought to give her a ring and find out what's going on. Don't you?"

"Yes," I agreed faintly, "I think I probably should. Thanks."

A few minutes later after a flurry of hurried goodbyes I finally put down the handset and sat in a rather dazed heap, wondering if that conversation had really just happened. Then, checking the time and seeing that Chaos would be in the middle of a lecture (assuming she was studying as she was supposed to be and not moonlighting as me on social media) I fired off a quick email suggesting that we needed to have a chat and asking her to ring me as soon as she was free.

Sticking the pretty little letter of congratulations that had triggered all this to the fridge with a magnet, I returned to

Redemption

the iPad determined to remember how to log into Facebook and find out what 'I' had been up to in recent weeks.

It was a most illuminating experience.

26. Skulduggery.
Definition: Secret activities conducted under the radar

*Remaining with the social media mystery in the **past**...*

A couple of hours later, as I was just putting a dish of lasagne into the oven for the evening's supper, a Skype call came into the iPad. I accepted it to find Chaos and Logic both looking at me from the one screen.

"Hi Mum!" they both chorused. "How are you?"

"You're together!" I said bluntly in surprise. They were supposed to be in different counties at different universities.

"Yup, I'm visiting Logic for the weekend," Chaos confirmed.

"That's nice," I said, deciding not to point out that it was only Wednesday (it was none of my business) and concentrated on how lovely it was that the two of them visited each other by choice. Although why I was surprised I didn't know, they've always been close.

"You wanted to chat," prompted Chaos.

"Oh yes, what's this about a book tour, and what on earth have you been posting on Facebook?"

"Just promotional stuff, I noticed you weren't logging in so I just thought I would run a Facebook ad for you. I'm an administrator on the page so it's easy enough to do. It's no big deal. It's reached quite a big audience already and has another two weeks to run. What do your sales figures look like? Has there been a response?"

"Well yes, I think so. I've definitely sold some, which is pretty incredible. I had no idea."

"That's good. The tour starts the week after the advert stops."

"Chaos, I can't possibly go on a book tour in two weeks' time. I know I don't have a job anymore, but I can't go travelling round the country at the drop of a hat. Who would look after your brothers? Your dad's working." I tailed off as I spotted that both girls were laughing. "What have I said?"

"It's not an *actual* book tour, Mum!" Chaos grinned.

"It's a virtual one," added Logic, as if that explained everything.

"What does that mean?" I demanded, trying not to get cross at my own ignorance.

"It means that your book will be hosted on a series of blogs and other websites all around the country, and you'll be interviewed and small sections of the first few chapters made available to try and drum up some interest in it," explained Chaos, looking exceedingly smug.

"What do I have to do?" I asked with mounting concern. I wasn't sure I liked the idea of being interviewed.

"Not much actually, I've organised most of it. I'll send you the interview questions. There aren't that many, so it won't take you long. Send them back to me when you are done and I'll send them on to the right sites. Then on each day of the tour you need to make sure you spend some time sharing posts, retweeting, blogging and reposting everything."

"You need to make sure you thank everyone who shares stuff about the book and retweets links too." Logic added as if it was the simplest thing in the world.

I felt rather sick. There was no way I could do that. I had barely been able to remember how to log in.

Spotting my look of mounting horror, Chaos said soothingly, "Don't worry Mum, I'll be home with you for the first two days of the tour and I'll show you what to do. I'll also share and post from my social media accounts too. It'll be fun."

"Sure it will," I answered with a studied nonchalance I did not feel, and then because it seemed expected, "Thank you."

"No worries, this is going to be great," smiled Chaos. "I'll see you in two weeks."

"We're off to the library now," said Logic.

"Yeah, and then the pub," said her sister. "Bye!"

With that the screen went blank and I wondered what on earth I was getting into. Then I thought about those little baby sales figures and the unexpected reviews and I couldn't help feeling a little fluttering of excitement. Perhaps Chaos was right, perhaps this could be fun.

27. Crepuscular
Definition: associated with the twilight hours

Returning to the present day, at a disgustingly early hour of the morning...

It was still dark, but as soon as I heard Quiet's bedroom door open I was wide awake. It was time to make my move.

Beloved Husband's plan was really simple. I was going to join Quiet for his morning travels; not follow him, not try to speak to him or question what he was up to, or even ask permission, I was to merely 'join' him as if it had been planned all along and see what happened.

Dragging on some tracksuit trousers over my pyjamas and grabbing a fleece, I slipped my feet into my trainers and padded down the stairs as silently as I could. Once in the kitchen, I took a mug out of the cupboard and placed it on the surface next to the one Quiet had just put out for himself. He looked at me for a few seconds before nodding faintly and dropping one tea bag into each mug. We didn't speak as the kettle boiled, nor as the tea bags were squashed, or the milk added.

Neither did we speak as we let ourselves out of the patio doors and wandered down the garden in the gentle silver-grey light of an almost Full Moon. We clambered over the fence at the bottom, taking care not to spill our drinks, and then headed off into the forest together.

It was beautiful, clear, cool, companionable and stunningly peaceful.

Alice May

We ambled a fair distance until we came to a stream where a tree had fallen some time ago; the trunk provided a convenient seat. This is where we parked ourselves and drank our tea together, listening to the sounds of the waking forest. Eventually as the light began to change and the sun started to rise, my son spoke.

"I miss it sometimes," he said in a low voice.

"What do you miss?" I whispered back.

"Being outside late at night and early in the morning. It's calm. It balances out all the things that happen in the day."

I waited for him to go on.

"I know it was a hard time for us all living in the tent in the garden, but it wasn't all bad. We were so much closer to nature and that was good."

I thought about it for a minute and I recalled the dancing bats in the trees and hedgehogs scurrying past the tent in the dusky evenings, the call of the owl at night and the fresh clear views of the moon. There was a magical beauty to being so close to nature and feeling the rhythm of the earth enfolding us at the start and end of each day.

"Yes," I confirmed softly, "Some of it was good."

Then he surprised me by speaking again.

"I think I'd like to do some camping this summer. Small said he'd like it too."

"Really?" I replied, "I thought none of you kids would ever want to camp again after what happened with the house." In fact, to tell you the truth, I'd spent many fruitless hours worrying about how all those events might have affected them.

He grinned at me, "Nah we're good. It happened, it's over, and we've moved on."

"I'm so glad you told me," I said with an answering smile. "As for camping, well that can be arranged."

We sat in silence for a bit longer before he nudged me gently and nodded further up the stream. Following his gaze, I could see movement. A deer was approaching the water to drink and, as she moved in the long grass, we could see that she was accompanied by a fawn.

"Oh, wow!" I muttered softly. I simply couldn't take my eyes off them but was aware of Quiet grinning at me.

"Just you wait till you see the badgers."

"There are badgers?" I whispered. "Where?"

"Next time," he promised in a low voice and turned back to look at the deer.

I tucked the delight that there was going to be a next time carefully into my heart with a contented sigh and watched my boy as he watched the deer. In that moment, I focussed on simply acknowledging just how much I adored him. How lucky I was to have him and all his siblings to cherish. As mums we can get so wrapped up in what is expected of us; the right way to be a parent. Making sure our children behave themselves, eat the right food, go to school, pass exams, conform with society's demands, turn up to music lessons, sports training and the rest of the whirl of everyday life. Yet somehow, in amongst all of that, it is vital that we take the time to just appreciate them for the wonderful miracles that they are.

Here was this lovely young man, who clatters through our home on his long limbs and tackles his brother at random moments before eating everything in sight whilst rarely saying a word, teaching me that taking a moment to simply sit and be, to acknowledge events for what they are and then move on, is so very important.

28. Coalescence:

Definition: the convergence of many elements to form a new whole

*Staying with the **present** day once again as this story finally draws to a close….*

Later that same day, in glorious contrast to our peaceful early morning, chaos was reigning in the kitchen. I mean the actual chaotic type of chaos in this case rather than my gorgeous grown-up-daughter-Chaos, although she was present too, singing loudly, and not necessarily accurately, along to something only she could hear, thanks to the happy application of ear buds. Logic was also singing only, unfortunately, it wasn't the same song, which made for an interesting 'mash up.' (Hark at me; I am so trendy, with my technical modern music terms!)

Both girls were sat at the breakfast bar supposedly doing university work on their laptops, although I had my doubts about that, as every so often one or other of them would suddenly laugh out loud at something for no obvious reason, leading me to conclude that they were probably studying but also on some form of social media at the same time. How their brains manage to multi task effectively like that is beyond me.

The boy Barbarians were indulging in a more physically demanding type of multi-tasking, enmeshed as they were in some sort of karate/judo/all-in-wrestling 'mash up' contest of their own, in the middle of the kitchen floor. It's a stone floor, so I was fairly sure some of those 'take-downs' must have smarted just a touch, although no one squealed and no bones seemed to have broken either. However, there was quite a lot of alarming grunting going on.

At the same time a large pan of something was bubbling furiously away on the stove. I wasn't sure what it contained or who had put it on but took the view that whoever it was hopefully knew what they were doing, so I was trying to ignore it.

In fact, I was doing my best to ignore everything. If I didn't acknowledge it then it couldn't possibly be happening, which is a technique I advise any mother to develop very early on in her maternal career. If no-one is actually dying, then there is no problem to stress about. Hence, I was sat at the conservatory table wearing headphones and ignoring everything. My headphones were of the big clumpy variety that were trendy way back in the dim and distant nineteen eighties but have come back into fashion again recently. I am sure you've seen them around, the sort that the youngsters of today think are a completely modern invention and hence 'cool' or 'sick' or 'rad' or whatever the word of the moment is for something that is 'on-trend'. (The up-to-date jargon changes so quickly I've given up trying to keep pace with it.) But really, we used to wear headphones like this decades ago back when 'cool' really meant…um…well… 'cool'!

However, I was not listening to music and I was definitely *not* singing along. I was trying to concentrate and was using the headphones more as ear defenders than anything else, as they proved very effective at cutting out the pandemonium my darling Barbarians were generating around me and which allowed me to focus on the laptop before me on the table. I was wading through what seemed like hundreds of emails that had arrived overnight.

Redemption

Interestingly enough they didn't seem the usual sort of miscellaneous junk from random sales companies, fraudulent enterprises and scam artists.

After ploughing through delivery confirmations from several online retailers and an online banking circular, I came across one from the nice lady in charge of the Literary and Creative Society evening event, thanking me for coming along and sharing my story. Apparently she had received some rather flattering feedback from the Society members and wanted to let me know. She finished her email by saying that she hoped I didn't mind but she had passed my particulars on to several other groups she knew who were always looking for good speakers. She felt that my signature talk was refreshingly different and entertaining that she was quite certain that other event organisers would be interested in contacting me. In fact, she suggested I would be 'snapped up'. It was really good to know that my presentation had been genuinely appreciated, not merely politely suffered by the audience.

Funnily enough the next three emails I read were inquiries about possibly booking me to speak at further events, so she hadn't been joking about passing on my details, or about there being a demand. The event organisers were obviously not hanging about.

This was quite exciting, and I had so effectively tuned out everything else that was going on around me that I didn't even hear the landline ringing stridently. None of the kids reacted to it either but then we've already discussed how they don't seem to bother with landlines, haven't we? If it's not mobile then it can't possibly be a phone. It was still ringing as Beloved Husband burst through the kitchen door.

Alice May

"Is anyone going to answer that phone?" he demanded. "I could hear it from outside." Looking up I watched him dump his jacket on the side and take a flying leap over the bundle of brawling boys on the floor to grab the handset before it stopped ringing. As I pulled my headphones off, I noticed that his aerial acrobatics act had successfully got everyone's attention and the noise level was significantly reduced almost immediately. (Perhaps he should do it more often!) The boys briefly stopped hammering at each other and the girls stopped caterwauling (ahem - I mean singing!), and all looked on with interest to see what he would do next.

"Hello?" he said, trying to catch his breath after such an unaccustomed burst of exercise. He was attempting to use his 'stern' voice, the one that was supposed to convey in a single word the fact that he would be most displeased if there was a cold caller on the other end of the line. We do seem to get quite a lot of those, so he has spent time perfecting this skill.

His eyes widened as he listened to the voice on the end of the line. Then he looked directly at me and started to frantically flap his hand in what I think was a request for complete silence. It was already quite quiet in the room so we all held our breath and waited.

"No, this is her personal assistant speaking. She's not available for a press interview just at this moment but you could email her, or alternatively I can take a message for her and she will get back to you."

He wiggled his fingers in the air, and his eyebrows too. Logic reacted by shoving a pad of paper and a pen under his hand

Redemption

so he could write down a name and number. Just as he was thanking the caller and hanging up the handset, my mobile started to buzz away next to me on the table. Picking it up, I saw a number I didn't recognise and swiped to answer it. A polite female voice enquired about booking me to speak at an art event for charity, at a fairly big venue, in the nearby town the following month. Flipping open my diary, I agreed, made a note of the particulars and ended the call, but my mobile started ringing again as soon as I tried to put it down. This time it was a lady from one of the local WI's asking if I could fill in for a speaker who had been forced to cancel at short notice due to ill health. The date she needed me was in two days' time. I agreed and again made a note in my diary. At the same time the shrill bleat of the main landline started up again. Giving me a quizzical look, Beloved Husband reached to answer it, just as I swiped to disconnect my mobile only for it to ring almost immediately once again.

Eventually we both got off the phones and just looked at each other.

"Well, you seem rather popular all of a sudden!"

"How bizarre!" I agreed.

"What was that about a press interview?" asked Logic.

"Not really sure, but I didn't hand the phone over to your mother when I realised it was a journalist because I don't think you can be too careful with the press. Best not get caught unprepared. He's going to send an email, which should give us an idea what he's after and allow you time to decide if you want to respond or not," he looked at me as he said this and shrugged.

"Yeah, that's wise," said Chaos, nodding thoughtfully.

"What about the other calls?"

"A couple of ladies want you to call them back, one about some book group and the other about a ladies' social event. I took names and numbers."

"Oh, that's nice, I'll give them a ring a bit later on."

"I think we'll have to assume that you are a bit of a hit!"

"So it would seem."

"You know, there might genuinely be something in this," said Chaos. "We might need to upgrade your website!"

"I have a website?" I asked in surprise.

"Oh yeah!" she admitted sheepishly, "didn't I tell you? I created it for your exhibition last year. We can probably expand it considerably now."

"What do you mean?"

"Business-wise. You are going to need a speaker's page with the details of your talk and upcoming events. You are going to charge to speak, aren't you?"

"Well, I thought I might charge a speaker's fee, plus a minimal mileage."

Redemption

"Good! That could prove to be a nice steady income stream, then there's a second potential income stream from the books that you will sell at these speaking events. Then there's the main income from your art work, in the form of exclusive original paintings, then prints, cards, inspirational quotes and the like. I can design you a whole online shop too, if you like. I'll have to take into account all the necessary regulations, the new data protection laws and security, so it might take a while." She started muttering about jpegs and dots per inch at that point so lost me quite quickly, but Logic seemed to be following her and nodded along as if she wasn't talking gibberish.

"She's right," agreed Beloved Husband, nudging me. "You have a ready-made market there. If you get regular speaking gigs, that'll give you a platform for the book and also your paintings. You have all the ingredients of a potentially successful business with three main elements to it, as an artist, an author and a speaker."

"Triangles are supposed to be the strongest geometric shapes," interjected the resident maths genius. We looked at her for clarification, "I'm just agreeing with you," Logic explained a touch defensively. "I think it could make a very effective business model, especially as it is all underpinned with a very positive human interest story. If the press are interested already, then you might even get some great publicity too."

"That's true, but PR is important, you'll have to think about your brand." Chaos looked even more thoughtful, if that were possible.

"Your accounts will be important too. You'll need to make sure you keep a record of all transactions. So you can pay the right tax. I'll do some research to find out the best way to do this," Logic said, turning to her laptop and typing furiously into it. The two girls started murmuring between themselves and enthusiastically making a list of all the things they thought I needed to consider.

"Perhaps this really is the perfect new job for you," rumbled Quiet thoughtfully, as Small broke free of the headlock he had absentmindedly held him pinned in for the last ten minutes, and delivered a swift kick to the back of his older brother's knees. Both boys tumbled to the ground and as I watched them, my thoughts went into freefall with all the potential possibilities.

"I think he might be right," agreed Beloved Husband. "It's a really good mix of your skills and so very creative which is a far cry from that job you've been doing all these years. I think you should go for it." There was a pause during which he reached over and took my hand gently and gave it a little shake to get me to look right at him. Then in a low voice that reached under the Barbarians babbling around us, "You know, with this and my new promotion we stand a real chance of turning our finances around."

I looked at him for a moment trying to work out if he was saying what I thought he was saying. "You mean….?"

He nodded. "Yes, I got the job. They told me just as I left the office this evening. You are looking at the new Director."

"Oh! Well done!" I flung my arms around him and hugged him tightly. "I am so proud of you."

Redemption

"And I am proud of you," he countered. "I think you should go for it. And I think we should do the other thing we mentioned too."

"You mean…" I could hardly dare say the words.

"Yes, I think I do."

"Really, can we?"

"Let's give it our best shot."

His smile was enough to have me launching myself at him again and throwing my arms around his neck. Laughing in absolute delight I said, "Can we do it now?" (Do get your mind out of the gutter please? I am not talking about that!)

He disentangled himself from my arms with a chuckle, "OK!" he said, "Just let me find a screwdriver. He opened the cutlery drawer and rummaged around a bit before he drew out a large yellow and black multi-headed screwdriver. Please don't ask me what it was doing in the cutlery drawer because I have no idea.

"Come on then gang, let's do this," he said, grabbing my hand and pulling me towards the front door.

29. Exhilaration

Definition: **A sensation of great happiness, excitement, elation.**

*Staying with the family in the **present** at this momentous instant……*

Realising something significant was afoot, the Barbarian girls abandoned their laptops and the Barbarian boys untangled themselves. All four of them followed us outside to the driveway where we interrupted Skelly doing some weeding in the front flower bed complete with a frilly apron, a wheelbarrow and a long-handled hoe.

Small ensured that Skelly took a break from his labours and joined us as we all stood around watching Beloved Husband, armed with his trusty screwdriver, advancing on the For Sale sign that still skulked over the hedge. He attacked the fixings anchoring the wooden pole supporting the board to our gatepost. After only a few moments though he gave a rude exclamation and chucked his screwdriver on the ground before heading determinedly for the garage.

Quiet stepped up to the gate to examine the fixings for a minute and then said knowledgeably, "Yup! The screws have sheered."

"That's a nuisance," agreed Small.

Logic shuffled over to me and asked, "Is Dad doing what I think he's doing?"

Redemption

"I hope so," I replied. "Otherwise I'm not quite sure what else he could be planning to do with that." I pointed at Beloved Husband who had re-emerged from the garage armed with a chainsaw trailing an extra-long electrical lead. He stalked right up to the Estate Agent board and started up his weapon before chopping right through the post holding it up. The board put up a token resistance but quickly gave in and toppled to the ground, as the noise of the chainsaw died away almost as soon as it had started.

"This is our home." Beloved Husband said defiantly. "We're staying right here!"

I couldn't help the warm happy tears that welled up in my eyes as I heard the huge cheer that erupted at his words from the Barbarians. There would be no more awful viewings and I could mess my studio up to my heart's content but, more importantly, we were going to stay in this crazy old/new house of ours, all the way out here in the middle of nowhere, in this incredible countryside with its forest full of deer and badgers; the home in which we had shared our lives so far and where, in spite of everything, we were so happy. It must be confessed that a certain amount of group hugging went on (yes, even the boys and Skelly) before we headed back inside, chattering and laughing together.

A short while later, armed with a celebratory cup of tea, I wandered out onto the patio. Sipping my drink thoughtfully, I surveyed the garden where we had lived in both tent and caravan for so long. The scuffed and damaged grass had recovered completely so that there was now no sign of either temporary residence. Towards the bottom of the garden on the gorgeous green grass, Skelly, now sporting full cricket whites including a helmet with a face guard and wicket-keeping gloves, was standing by a set of cricket stumps complete with bails resting on top, no doubt waiting for the boys to come and play with him.

The sun was shining and bright, cheerful birdsong hung in the warm air as I surveyed the peaceful scene. Looking back at the house I thought of all that had passed to bring me to this moment and I really wished that for just one instant I could go back in time to the old me standing on the drive watching the walls of my home disintegrate before my eyes. I wanted to give that poor broken mother a hug and say 'it's going to be all right! It's going to be horrible for a bit, and there are going to be times when you think this is going to destroy you, but it won't. You are stronger than you think. You can do it. Your husband and children will be fine, and you won't believe where all this is ultimately going to take you, so hang in there.'

I was a very different person now from the one I used to be, as a direct result of what happened the day my house sat down. That self-knowledge gave me courage. Sometimes, in the very depths of darkness, a small glimmer of light can effectively guide the way. My art had enabled me to express my deepest feelings without having to find words and then, when I was getting better, the words had found me and a story was born. I had a tale to tell and there were people asking to hear it. This wasn't about me, but about sharing a story; something human beings have been doing for thousands of years.

We weren't the only family to have come up against a difficult situation. There were, no doubt, countless other people just like us out there, struggling to hold families together against impossible odds. Life can throw countless difficulties into the path to trip us up and sometimes we simply don't feel we have the resilience we need. The obstacles before us can seem impossible to overcome. Hearing about another person's journey through a tricky time can potentially cast new light on otherwise apparently insurmountable situations.

Let us not forget that in order for a mighty oak to grow, first a tiny seed must fall and become buried in the earth. It must then fight to find a way through the darkness to reach sunlight in order to live. I had survived the collapse of the house and then battled my way through the darkness of both the emotional turmoil and the physical strain of the subsequent situational fall out. Now, having germinated and broken through the surface of the earth like a tiny sapling, I had found the strength to develop and grow, nurtured by the knowledge that I was a survivor. All I had to do now was to move forward in that new strength and understanding. Knowing the direction that I wanted to travel in and having the drive to take the first steps was immensely empowering. What seemed initially like a first tiny baby step was proving, in fact, to be quite momentous. I felt energised and motivated and completely driven to succeed at my goal.

I could bind my paintings with my book, and now my speaking into the same package, each supporting the other. After all these years I could genuinely call myself an artist. It wasn't going to be easy, I had a lot of hard work ahead of me, but I was certain that I could do it. I had changed and was still changing as a direct result of what had happened, and I was beginning to respect and even to like the person I was becoming. How extraordinary! I had never felt like that before.

Alice May

Who would have thought that such a long-held childhood dream to pursue a creative career would finally come true at the ripe old age of 46? Perhaps the spirit of my grandmother was watching over me, with a smile on her face saying 'At last, my girl, it's about time you followed your dream! Even if it took the house falling on you to make you recognise it.'

Smiling at my mental musings, I shook my head.

Turning towards the house I could see that the girls had brought their laptops out onto the patio and were settling into the comfy chairs there to type companionably away together in the sunshine. Then the sound of running feet and laughter heralded the arrival of both boys, at speed now, equipped with cricket bat and ball, tripping and tumbling over each other on their way to join Skelly at the crease.

I looked at my Barbarians and wondered where their dreams would take them.

Behind the boys, at a more dignified pace, came Beloved Husband, ambling over the grass with his own cup of tea in hand. On reaching me, he put his free arm around my shoulders and we stood together in the cool shade of the old oak tree and looked at our house; a house that, like us all, had been through the wars yet was still a home in which our little family could flourish

There we all were; the slightly barmy but happy family from the house that sat down.

Epilogue

And there we shall leave our heroine, dear reader, at the end of one incredible journey and the beginning of the next. She is content in the company of her crazy but fabulous family as the whole tribe are reunited, complete with skeleton, to enjoying the summer sunshine together.

None of us know what the future will bring but the fact that everything is alright in this one perfect moment, right here, right now, is a blessing that we should not overlook.

There is a saying that time heals. I wonder if that is true or perhaps time merely enables one to gain some perspective; the ability to see events from a more holistic point of view, a change in perception facilitating a greater understanding of the bigger picture. None of us exists as an island and all events are inextricably linked. Perhaps time allows the brain to process information, to permit the marrying of an emotional response with a more practical or philosophical one. I don't know. Sadly, some hurts never heal, and we have to learn to live with them somehow, but the making of irrevocable decisions whilst in the grip of major emotional responses should always be avoided until distance and perspective can be gained.

Our heroine has certainly been through the mill, but who hasn't in life? The overall outcome of these events has been a good one, in spite of everything. Her house may have sat down, and her security might have been torn apart, but she has grown stronger and a little bit wiser in the aftermath. The yin and yang of life has achieved a balance once again.

It always does in the end.

Alice May

Redemption

Definition:
The action of regaining something that was lost.

Alice May

Barbarian Boys Favourite 'Special' Fried Rice

Ingredients
Whatever you can find in the fridge that hasn't gone off
Eggs, beaten with a little milk if you have it but not if you don't
Rice freshly boiled, and drained
Soy sauce
Pepper

Directions
Chop up whatever you found in the fridge (that hasn't gone off like onions, peppers, ham/bacon/chicken etc.) really small and fry in a wok until cooked through.

Then beat however many eggs you have (the more eggs the merrier in the Barbarian Boys' opinion), chuck in a bit of soy sauce and add to the wok, plus a slug of milk to stop it all drying out and stir. Keep stirring.

Then once the eggs start to scramble, add the rice and keep it moving until the eggs are cooked through and everything is heated through thoroughly and nice and hot. Add pepper to season but no salt as the soy sauce is salty enough.

This really is just a way to feed teenagers when you've run out of almost anything and everything, but you are unable to (or can't be bothered to) go to a shop to buy something more suitable. Fortunately, my boys love it. Beloved Husband is less enamoured but then he can always shift for himself, can't he?

Alice May

Making a four foot snowman without snow

You will need:
Gardening gloves plus wire cutters
Chicken wire plus extra thin wire for fixing
Flour
Water
Strips of newspaper or waste paper (Your old GCSE notes are good for this, assuming you passed and don't need to re-sit of course)
Tissue paper or paint
Orange card cut into a semi-circle and rolled up to make a nose resembling a carrot
Two black buttons for eyes. PVA glue
Plenty of time to clean up

Directions
Using the gardening gloves to protect your hands, bend the chicken wire into the shape of a snowman's body and head and then fix in place with bits of thin wire.

Mix flour and water using half and half quantities until you have a runny white mess. Dip in strips of paper and lay over the chicken wire frame. Build up several layers and then leave to dry. Do try not to indulge in a soggy wet paper fight with your partner in crime at this point as the results will be fairly disastrous. Once dry, you can either paint the colour of your choice or stick scrunched up tissue paper all over your snowman.

Add eyes and nose, then hat, scarf and pipe. Enjoy!

What happened to Skelly?

In case you were wondering, Skelly has found a degree of fame in recent times. He now has a job at the local sixth form college where he happily divides his time between the biology laboratory, assisting with anatomy lectures, and the art department where he is employed as a model for the life (?) drawing class.

Nevertheless, he still spends the school holidays advising Beloved Husband on his latest gardening obsession (he is currently attempting to grow a wide variety of vegetables that Small will no doubt refuse to eat), and occasionally deigns to act as a sophisticated scarecrow sporting a wide variety of Harry Potter inspired outfits.

Ultimately though, his favourite occupation is always going to be that of loafing around at the house that sat down. He can generally be located at the bottom of the garden, under a large floppy hat, lounging in a hammock in the sunshine with a good book. He is often accompanied by a four-foot papier-mâché snowman.

About the Author
Alice May

Alice May is a huge advocate for self-care and resilience through creative activities and speaks regularly on the subject to a wide variety of groups.

She is a working mother with four not-so-small children and she is fortunate enough to be married to (probably) the most patient man on the planet. They live in, what used to be, a ramshackle old cottage in the country.

Her conservatory is always festooned with wet washing and her kitchen full of cake. She loves listening to the radio.

Inspired by true-life events (their house really did fall down) and fuelled by some really frantic painting sessions, this story wouldn't leave her alone until it was written.

She hopes you enjoy it.

If you have any comments about this book please send them to: alicegmay@hotmail.com
Website: www.alicemay.weebly.com
Twitter: @AliceMay_Author
Or find Alice May's author page on Facebook.
Alternatively, you can see Alice May paint on YouTube by searching for 'Alice May Artist'.

P.S. Please note that no Barbarians, skeletons or snowmen were harmed during the writing of this book.

Talks by Alice May

'Surviving The House That Sat Down!'

'Surviving The House That Sat Down' is Alice May's signature presentation. It is a positive and uplifting talk based on the events of three years ago when Alice's house partially collapsed one day and she and her husband and 4 children were forced to move into a tent in the garden. They were on the verge of losing everything.

It was shocking! And yet it was not the end of the world. Amazing things can come from disaster.

As a direct result of what happened that day, Alice is now happier than she has ever been before.

She used that homeless scenario as the inspiration for her first two independent fictional novels. These books have gone on to win two independent book awards (Chill with a Book Awards; www.chillwithabook.com).

Using her own personal artwork as illustration, Alice's signature talk gives a flavour of her inspiring journey from the ruins of her home to her life now as a published author, artist and public speaker.

For more information go to www.alicemay.weebly.com

Chasing Rainbows – Dreams can come true

See the paintings from The House That Sat Down!

In this second presentation, Alice May artist and award-winning author of 'The House That Sat Down' series, discusses the healing power of art and creativity, whilst sharing a selection of her own original art and video painting demonstrations.

The world is an increasingly stressful place and it is so important that we find ways to deal with the pressures of everyday life. Find out about the many different types of art therapy available to us today. Hear some of the theories on why it can be so effective and learn about the women who influenced the early development of art as a therapy.

This presentation uses Alice's personal experience of the healing power of art, an inspirational story that has enabled her dreams to come true.

Details of all Alice's talks as well as her books and artwork can be found on the website.

www.alicemay.weebly.com

Redemption

Read on to meet two of the amazingly supportive women behind the characters in my story.

Gill Donnell (MBE) aka 'Lady Awesome'

"Behind every successful woman is a tribe of other successful women who always have her back."

Networking is a powerful tool and an important element in any marketing for business.

The Successful Women in Business Network is THE business networking meeting for women in the South West. Gill holds monthly business networking events for women across Devon, Dorset, Somerset & Hampshire.

https://www.womensdevelopment.co.uk/

Beverley Hepting aka 'Magenta'
The Message Maestro

Bev is an award-winning speaker and coach who will work with you, transforming your business by clarifying your message, allowing you to speak in public with confidence and clarity.

https://bevhepting.com/

Alice May